"I have a different solution. One that would address *both* problems."

And here was the thing he'd clearly been reluctant to bring up, even as he'd made up his mind. Monica braced herself for anything. Something about Andrea consumed her, as if finally, she had tuned in to the right frequency of her own heart and body. "What's the solution?"

"We will pretend that the story the tabloid press made up is true. In two days, we'll arrive at a charity gala together. That will be enough of an announcement that we are together."

Try as she might, Monica couldn't muster up a response. Shock enveloped her so fully that all she could do was freeze and stare and...

Pretend they were together, that they'd been in a relationship for months. Go to a party with him. Pretend like she had the right to touch him, and kiss him and want him...

Suddenly, she felt feverish all over again.

Tara Pammi can't remember a moment when she wasn't lost in a book—especially a romance, which was much more exciting than a mathematics textbook at school. Years later, Tara's wild imagination and love for the written word revealed what she really wanted to do. Now she pairs alpha males who think they know everything with strong women who knock that theory and them off their feet!

Visit the Author Profile page
at Harlequin.com for more titles.

FIANCÉE FOR THE CAMERAS

TARA PAMMI

Harlequin

PRESENTS

Harlequin® PRESENTS™

ISBN-13: 978-1-335-93920-3

Fiancée for the Cameras

Harlequin Enterprises ULC
22 Adelaide St. West, 41st Floor
Toronto, Ontario M5H 4E3, Canada
www.Harlequin.com

Printed in Lithuania

Recycling programs for this product may not exist in your area.

MIX
Paper | Supporting responsible forestry
FSC® C021394

FIANCÉE FOR THE CAMERAS

For Soraya—my fabulous new editor—for giving me new energy for so many more delicious Harlequin Presents books. I can't believe we're already at three books! Here's to many more together.

CHAPTER ONE

HER BRIDEGROOM WASN'T COMING.

Monica D'Souza realized the awful dawning truth even as she dialed Francesco's number one more time. It continued to ring, as it had done over the past hour, and with each unanswered call, she was beginning to feel like something a careless tourist had chewed up and spat over the steps of the piazza.

Or worse, something forgotten or abandoned. Or both. Which she'd already experienced far too many times in her life.

Had Francesco been in an accident? He drove that moped pretty recklessly, and Monica could just imagine him bleeding out on some tiled floor a few streets away. Why else would he not only be late but also not even call her? He *had to* be indisposed in some way. He had to.

Standing outside the marvelous Sala Degli Specchi hall in Palazzo Reale for the past two hours—because of course she had to arrive at least an hour early—in the elaborate puffy white dress that she had bought online, she was beginning to draw attention of the worst kind.

The dress was nothing like the website posting had said, with a cheap, plasticky feel to the fabric and worse, a weirdly pungent chemical smell that was beginning to make her feel faint.

Breaking all her rules, she'd stolen a sachet of lavender from her boss's private bathroom at work and pressed it between the folds. But the smell of the dress was as tenacious as she was and now it clung to her skin, creating her very own scent of desperation.

Granted, she hadn't paid a lot for the dress—not after putting the little nest of her savings from the past three and a half years into the tiny studio flat she and Francesco wanted to move into later this week.

A new home, though it was tiny, a new life, with someone who wanted to be with her... It was all she'd ever dreamed of.

With a frustrated exhale, Monica pushed away the ridiculous veil that had come with the dress out of her eyes, blinking back prickly tears. The June sun beat down mercilessly, probably melting her sunscreen and makeup. All she needed now was mascara tracks running down her cheeks to complete the picture of the ghastly, pathetic bride.

No, she refused to believe that Francesco would do this to her. She'd seen him only last night and while there had been a desperation to his kisses and more than usual urgency to his demands about making love to her, he'd said he couldn't wait to begin their life together.

She had only known him two months but discovered they had so much in common. They were both orphans and had grown up in care homes all over the country— she in the US and he in Italy—and they both wanted desperately to build a family, both eager for belonging. Like her, Francesco loved art and history and languages, and on their first meeting they had chatted for hours and at the end of it, she'd been absolutely head over heels in love. And he had expressed with that European flair that he felt the same toward her.

Over the next few weeks, she'd seen him at least three times a week, the only impediment to their relationship being her very demanding boss and the rigorous work schedule he imposed on her as his assistant.

Monica had been floating on cloud nine, so much that even *he*—of the brooding glower, grumpy manners and workaholic energy—had noticed and questioned her.

Then, a week ago, Francesco had proposed to her right in this very spot, his grin that charming, naughty one that had tempted her more than once into almost breaking her rule that she'd only have sex when she was fully ready.

She'd always been a little dull, averse to risk. Dependable, definitely. She would have liked to spend, and would have spent, her entire life under the radar if not for the fact that whoever had abandoned her to an orphanage when she'd been a baby had passed on genes that made her "stunning" and "beautiful."

While she could appreciate the symmetry of her angular features, her golden-brown complexion and the uniqueness of her yellow, catlike eyes, her face and body had always drawn attention of the worst kind, first from boys in all the foster homes she'd bounced through and then men—even the ones who were supposed to protect a homeless teen.

But her face had drawn Francesco to her. Francesco, who was fun and charming and sexy. She took everything too seriously and he took it very easy, breezing through life, making bets upon bets. No wonder he was late now. She wouldn't be surprised if he'd gotten caught up in arranging a fun surprise for her or some other daring activity for their honeymoon.

He's only late, she kept telling herself.

Not dumping her here. Not leaving her like everyone eventually did. Not deciding that something else was more important than her.

More than one woman had given her a piteous look and more than one man had whistled, laughed and asked if she wanted to celebrate a wedding night without getting married. After studying Italian for two years at a community college in New York and living in Milan for four years now, she had a good grasp of the language.

She wiped at the beads of sweat over her upper lip and licked her parched lips. Opening her small backpack, she was pulling out her water bottle when her cell phone chirped.

"Francesco? You're late," she said, unable to keep a sliver of frustrated anger out of her tone. "Our appointment was for an hour ago but I've sorted it out with them. If you can—"

"I'm sorry, *mia cara*. A golden opportunity came up for my business and you know how hard I've been working to get cash infusion, *si*?"

"I do," Monica said, blinking a mixture of tears and makeup out of her eyes. "And I fully support you," she added softly, as compensation for her miserable tone. "But I'm waiting for you. At the Palazzo Reale. To get married."

"Ahh…*bella*. Unfortunately, this opportunity means I have to postpone the wedding. At least for a year."

Unfortunately…

Misery and pain swamped Monica, bringing her back to that time the public school she'd attended had gone on a trip to swamplands in sixth grade. The whole trip to Florida, she'd been reminded by most of her classmates that she was the charity case their parents had chipped in extra for. She hadn't cared—it was the first time she was seeing something other than the orphanage and foster homes and her school—but then Olivia Kent had pushed her head down into the water because Timothy Evans had smiled at Monica and not her.

This felt exactly like that. Like she couldn't breathe.

"I don't understand. What does your business opportunity have to do with our getting married? You know how much I support all your dreams. If you want, I'll even ask my boss for a loan if you really—"

"No need. You didn't want to ask before, *si*? Now I don't need that big shot Valentini's help. This whole marriage thing was your idea."

"What? That's not true. You proposed to me. You wanted us to get that flat to live together. You made me shell out—"

"*Basta!* I will return your puny money. I'm not a man who depends on a woman. Especially one so clingy and needy. All the time, you are cooking and doing my laundry and offering your services up. A man can get confused when a woman throws herself at him like that. I only thought you were a good goose after—"

Monica felt like she was getting whiplash, and it wasn't her dress or the sun beating down on her. Francesco thought she was...*clingy and needy.* He thought she had thrown herself at him. He thought...

Of course, Francesco didn't love her. Or at least not

more than himself and his business ventures. Not when loving her meant giving up bigger, better opportunities. Not when it was inconvenient. Maybe what he felt for her wasn't love at all.

"You are a beautiful woman with a sexy body. You always smile and maintain good cheer. I thought hey, she is a hot American woman with good connections in Milan. But it was convenience, Monica. Especially since you don't even give out sex. If you still want to celebrate our wedding night without—"

Hands shaking, Monica hung up and fought the maddening urge to throw her cell phone across the steps into the cheerful fountain.

No. She couldn't. It was her work phone and there was no point in taking her misery out on it when she'd have to fish it out of the fountain, then get a replacement, then explain to the IT department how it had fallen into the water in the first place. And God forbid if the phone got clogged up with water and she missed a call from her very demanding, very important, boss.

Especially today of all days, when Mr. Valentini might well announce his engagement to his ex, Mrs. Chiara Rossi. She'd been expecting it for more than six weeks now, given the impending merger between Valentini Luxury Goods and Chiara's father's company, Brunetti Leathers. Especially ever since she'd run into Mrs. Rossi at a dinner party and had been warned off setting her sights on her boss.

Hurriedly, she made sure the ringer was turned up all the way.

This was her, she thought, tears falling down her cheeks, with an edge of hysteric laughter setting into the sound. This woman, who minutes after being dumped at the altar—though technically it was city hall—balked at the idea of even throwing her phone because it might give rise to unnecessary questions and inconvenience for someone else. Especially the man to whom she owed so much.

But even the usual nerve-racking urgency she felt around Mr. Valentini wasn't enough to cut through the weight of her misery, which sank through her belly as if she'd swallowed one of Francesco's enormous dumbbells.

This was her—Monica D'Souza—once again alone in the world, with no place to go, once again abandoned and unwanted.

Andrea Valentini, CEO of Valentini Luxury Goods, did not usually involve himself in the personal lives of his employees. He could barely remember their full names and personal situations. All he did remember was their abilities and efficiencies and how loyal they were to his company. He didn't need to know more than that. And he didn't have the bandwidth to know more than that. Which was why he, nearly two years ago, when another assistant had quit on him, had jumped on the opportunity to promote his mother's rescuer, the walking, talking human resource machine that was Monica D'Souza.

He prided himself on seeing people for who they were and once again, he'd been right. During her convalescence at the hospital after she'd saved his mother from a dangerous mugger, Andrea had seen the magic Ms. D'Souza could weave with numbers and interpersonal affairs.

Offering her a job as one of his junior assistants in

exchange for saving his mother's life had been a small price to pay. As he'd expected, her sharp mind and her extraordinary talent in dealing with people who always needed something from him, which meant he could actually focus on the business, had had her climbing the corporate ladder super-fast. Until he'd had no choice but to steal her for himself exclusively.

Now Ms. D'Souza pretty much ran his professional life, and his personal life, too, though he didn't really have one. She made him an approachable package for the media, for his shareholders and even for his own family.

He'd never really had any complaints about her, until a few weeks ago when she'd met Francesco Ricci—a charming conman Andrea could scent a kilometer away. How Ms. D'Souza didn't see his true character was a mystery to him.

While it had irritated the hell out of him to see her throw her breathtaking smiles and her generous compliments at such a rascal, Andrea had set her little flirtation out of his mind. She was not only naive but also young at just twenty-three. She deserved to have fun, even if it was with a rogue who didn't deserve to kiss her little toe.

Except his mother had called his attention to the fact that Francesco had not only proposed to Ms. D'Souza but he had also talked her into giving up her savings to finance some ridiculous hovel he wanted to rent, a week ago.

On impulse, Andrea had had his chauffeur drive him to that dingy, unsafe neighborhood, only to realize that Francesco had fleeced Ms. D'Souza. If it was just that, Andrea could have called in his connections and had him hauled to prison.

But no, Francesco had found his golden goose in Ms. D'Souza and meant to fleece her for the rest of his life. Especially with her close connection to his own family. That, Andrea could not allow.

So here he was, after having one of his associates pay off the thug to dump Ms. D'Souza. And while it was cruel, Andrea hoped this would cure Ms. D'Souza of her naive faith in every scoundrel she came across. The woman needed a crash course in the reality of people.

But of course, it wasn't enough that Andrea had taken care of the mess she'd gotten herself into. Mama wanted him to make sure Ms. D'Souza was okay in the aftermath, when the last thing he needed was a distraught woman on his hands.

As if his ex's machinations to force him into accepting her as his wife as a bonus prize along with the merger with her father's company wasn't bad enough.

Once, Andrea would have done anything—*had* done anything—to win Chiara's hand and heart. But she had chosen a different man, a man more suited to give her the lifestyle she was used to and the kind of commitment she'd wanted. Her gamble hadn't paid off quite the way she'd foreseen, for her husband had failed at a few business ventures before dying in an accident.

And now his mother, and Chiara's father and Chiara herself apparently expected him to pick up where they had left off ten years ago and enter wedded bliss with her. Or the merger wouldn't go through, her father had the gall to say, when Andrea hadn't immediately jumped on the condition.

The very thought made his temper boil over. The fact that Brunetti now tied the fate of this merger—a

merger Andrea had sunk everything into—to his marrying Chiara…

As of now, Andrea had no solution to a problem that
was suddenly a big headache. He wanted to say no without saying no, without upsetting the delicate balance
that was his business negotiations with Chiara's father.

He leaned back in the car, gritting his teeth, and found
his mind drifting to Ms. D'Souza. Suddenly, it didn't feel
like such a chore to rescue her from the clutches of the
rogue. At least with her, Andrea knew there was no hon-
eyed trap, no sweet nudges toward the altar. Nothing but
painfully naive honesty packaged in a goddess's body.

Monica flipped through the few contacts on her phone,
holding up the train of her dress high off the ground,
even as she felt a slow, relentless burning across the skin
of her upper back.

After calling Francesco a few more times and finding
it going straight to voice mail, she'd just been standing
there feeling lost. Unraveled. Facing the very real truth
of her situation—she had nowhere to go.

After plucking her water bottle out of her bag, she took
the last sip and pressed the cool metal to her cheek. She
wanted to rip the dress off her skin and jump into the
fountain herself. Drench herself from head to foot in the
cool water. Wash off this nasty day. Would anyone stop
her? Was the last event on this crazy day to be arrested
for public indecency in Milan of all places?

Letting the hem fall to the ground, she peeked over
her shoulder to see why the skin on her back felt like
someone had lit up a matchstick and pressed it unrelent-
ingly against it.

She couldn't see much. Blinking, feeling a strange nausea well up at the back of her throat, she frowned. It was summer in Milan, so yes, it was hot. But she'd never felt this…scorching sensation on her skin before, nor this lightheadedness. Something was wrong.

There was only one person she could call, only one person who had been unflinchingly kind to her for close to four years now. Mrs. Valentini would welcome her with open arms, and yet, Monica felt the strangest reluctance. Everything Flora knew, her older son would be made aware of. The thought of Andrea Valentini finding out what a pathetic mess she was made the scorching burn on her back feel like a cool glaze.

Suddenly, a very familiar Bugatti with tinted windows came into view at the end of the street and Monica stiffened. Any doubt she might have had turned into dust when the chauffeur parked the car right in front of the huge steps leading to the Palazzo Reale, uncaring of whom he was blocking.

As if his boss belonged there.

Because he did.

And Monica knew that her nightmare had one last cringeworthy humiliation to deliver. Her day wasn't over yet.

CHAPTER TWO

SHE SHOULD HAVE looked pathetic.

If Andrea was honest with himself, she did, a little. But standing on those steps, with people watching her and mocking her, in that ghastly overpuffed, overlaced, frothy concoction that someone like Chiara wouldn't let a staff member wear in her household, Ms. D'Souza also looked brave. As if she'd entered a battle and lost it spectacularly, and yet somehow remained full of that fierce little heart he had never seen in anyone else.

He should have sent his chauffeur, Pascale, to pick her up, throw her over his shoulder if she offered her useless, prideful resistance and dump her inside the car and speed off, so that he could leave her piteous…situation in Mama's capable, caring hands.

But a little something went off track—a little blip in the fold of the universe, as his brother was fond of saying—and Andrea decided to get out of the car and pick up the wretched baggage himself.

That little lift of her chin as Monica's catlike golden eyes met his when he lowered the tinted window— even as her hands trembled at her sides, even as her face looked like it was made of myriad shades of red and brown and gold with a little green around her mouth thrown in for good measure, even as she looked like a jilted bride who had crawled out of some haunted mansion in a cheap gothic novel—was the thing that provoked some base instinct that Andrea had never known existed in him.

He raised a hand to his chauffeur to turn the car around on the busy junction, aware that they were already attracting attention. Usually, he hated spectacles like this. He was a well-known figure in Milan and his face was the one that had turned a small leather goods company into his current billion-dollar machine that had resuscitated a sinking economy on its last breath. Flexing his power and prestige and connections in this way had never been his style.

But something egged him on and he didn't even calculate the risk like he usually did when he encountered such a situation.

He finally reached his assistant and felt a sharp spike of awareness as she looked down at him from a few steps above. Whatever hairstyle she'd started the day with had unraveled, leaving her silky brown waterfall of hair falling to her waist. Her skin was flushed and blotched at the same time, as if she'd been trekking in the sun without water for too long. Her lips were chapped and she kept licking them.

Even with the overdone lace puffs at her shoulders and too much lace fluttering at her neckline, the bodice paid homage to her high breasts and then nipped tightly at her tiny waist. How she had managed to find a dress that fell too far to the ground when she was so tall, Andrea would never know. His leisurely traversing revealed a tear at the hem and one at the waistline, as if she had pulled and torn at the dress to get it away from her body.

But what alarmed Andrea when he would have otherwise found the whole thing comically tragic was the reddish flush to her cheeks, her neck and the skin beneath. And the way she couldn't seem to stop trembling.

She looked like she was unraveling, providing a spectacle for bored tourists and Milanese alike.

The stubborn tilt of her chin was gone. Had he imagined it, the little flicker of bravery? Was she that same lost little lamb who gave foolishly and generously of herself to one and all?

"Come, let's go," he said when he reached her, employing his usual brisk tone, hoping to devolve whatever emotional outburst was building inside the woman like a damn geyser. The last thing he wanted was to be near her when it erupted.

Have a little care, Andrea. She's twenty-three years old, years younger than you in age and experience and she just got dumped.

Suitably chastened, as if Papa were standing next to him and speaking those words, Andrea extended a hand toward her. "There is no point in lingering here, Ms. D'Souza."

"I can't, Mr. Valentini," she said, her usually husky voice paper-thin. "At least not until I get this thing off me."

Andrea frowned. He tried, *tried his best*, to modulate his tone but he was now regretting the impulse of getting out of his car at all. This had disaster written all over it, for her and him. "You're very well aware of how much I loathe public scenes, Ms. D'Souza. It is bad enough that

Mama wouldn't leave me alone until I picked you up here and delivered you to her care. Bad enough that I had to come here all the way from Mr. Brunetti's estate at the outskirts of the city. You're also well aware how busy this week has been at work and how much your leave today has inconvenienced me already. Enough with your—"

"All I need is that Swiss blade you keep on yourself all the time," she said, eyes not only watering but also shedding tears, which were running tracks down her cheeks and into the grooves of her delicate clavicle.

Cristo, the woman was stunning and sensuous even when she was a hot garbage mess, as one of his younger cousins was fond of saying. Now Ms. D'Souza was swaying where she stood and Andrea thought she might disappear in a whiff of smoke if he so much as breathed wrong.

"Then you can turn around, forget this little scene ever happened and return to your air-conditioned suite and that Brunetti contract. If you do me this favor, I'll even put in a few hours of work tonight. And I'll return the blade back to you. I know it is a cherished gift from Mrs. Rossi."

Andrea stilled, shocked at her request. Shocked at how much of his personal life she was privy to. That he held on to the blade that Chiara had gifted him almost a decade ago, not even his mother knew. It had been foolish sentimentality at the beginning. And now he was simply attached to the master craftsmanship of the blade. Not that he had to explain his uncharacteristic fondness of the blade to this woman.

"Do not be ridiculous, Ms. D'Souza. I'm not so much of a monster that I would make you come in to work when you're in such a…pathetic state." It was a bad choice of word, yet again. Andrea regretted it the moment it found shape, even before it landed and she flinched.

Dio mio, what was wrong with him? He was called ruthless, arrogant, but casual cruelty had never been his weapon of choice.

She did draw her chin up then and he knew he hadn't imagined the same earlier. "If you're not going to help me, leave me in peace."

"What good will a Swiss blade do you now? You should have taken better care with your money and your heart before you trusted such a scoundrel. All these dramatics are of no use. Walking naked through these streets is not going to bring him back."

"That's not what I mean to do at all," she said, mouth falling open at his suggestion. "Wait, how do you know that he…" Closing her eyes, she took a bracing breath.

Once again, Andrea was struck by her quiet dignity.

She rubbed a hand over her cheek and neck and opened her eyes. There was a flatness to her gaze that he disliked intensely. "You know what? Like you said, it doesn't matter. Francesco dumping me here has no more or no less significance just because you found out and use it to talk down to me. If you'll excuse me, I have other things to take care of. I'm sorry that Flora inconvenienced you and I will see you tomorrow morning at work."

He should have let her go, let *it* go. In fact, he was glad to see she had some backbone. But he didn't. Apparently, today was full of surprises.

When she sidestepped him to take the stairs down past him, he grabbed her wrist. "I'm not talking down to you," he said, stubbornly wanting the last word. "And you are…"

His words stilled. She was burning to his touch.

Andrea dropped her wrist and touched the back of his hand to her forehead and then her neck, like he had seen Mama do countless times.

"Are you dehydrated?" he demanded, pushing into her space, touching her compulsively in a few more spots. "You're flushed and sweating and…you need a doctor. You're a stubborn creature to stand here and argue with me when you—"

"I need your blade," she said, shoving away from him. "If you have even a tiny bit of respect for me, you'll listen to me when I say I know what I need. Now, Andrea."

It was how she said his name that convinced him. With an easy familiarity, as if she had said it many times. When in reality, he had always been Mr. Valentini—his last name almost a shield. Now, in that low-pitched husky voice, it sounded intimate and strangely like something he had imagined before.

"I will not let you do anything foolish, Monica." Her own name fell easily, effortlessly, from his lips. As if some hitherto closed door had been unlocked, never to be shut again. *Cristo*, the heat must be getting to him, too, because that was a load of bullshit if he'd ever heard, in his own head.

She scoffed then, and he felt the loss of her innocence keenly. "I have lived through too many shitty foster homes, evaded too many incoming hits, fought too many roving hands, to now harm myself over a man who has no…loyalty."

He placed his blade into her outstretched hand. "You're

an orphan, then?" How had he not known it in two years of working together so closely? Or the nearly four years that she'd been close to his mother and brother? How had he compartmentalized this woman so easily?

She didn't answer and Andrea knew that it was a choice, that he hadn't made the cut to her inner circle. Damn if it didn't irritate the hell out of him.

She palmed the blade, as if to test its weight and slant, and then turned the pointed edge toward the bodice. Andrea nearly leaped at her, his pulse jumping into his throat. Only to realize that she meant to rip the bodice off her flesh.

"Put some pressure on my hand," she said, and he clamped his fingers over hers automatically. "The zipper is stuck."

She was different now, her calm voice and the rigid resolve showing something else beneath the soft-spoken, highly efficient shadow he'd gotten used to for years.

Too close, they were too close. Any protest he had that they were creating a spectacle disappeared as he noted the slight swelling of her lips and the small reddish bubbles near her neck. Her eyes flickered for a second, meeting his, then she groaned as the fabric finally rent under their combined pressure. It fell open, revealing an ivory white lacy bra that was clearly much more expensive than the cheap dress. Her breasts were thrust up, falling and rising with her labored breaths.

"Now the back, please," she said, and turned around, presenting him with her back.

Shaking himself out of the sudden haze, Andrea cut through the fabric of the dress in the back. He'd barely gotten it down to her waist when she ripped it off her skin as if it…burned her.

He saw it then. The angry red rash all over her back, dipping all the way to the slope of her buttocks. A combination of blisters and rash that looked…intensely painful. Alarmed, Andrea pushed the dress down her shoulders and then down her waist and hips. He pulled the bra away from her skin and cut through that, too, realizing now that her skin must burn when anything touched that ghastly rash in this heat. He hated himself a little for making her wait so long before listening to her.

"That feels…better," she said, turning around and burrowing her upper body into his. The blaze of heat from her body nearly seared him. Her hands were shaking as she held the torn dress against her breasts, her mouth a rictus of pain, her eyes cloudy.

"You'll be fine now, Ms. D'Souza," he said stiffly, shrugging off his jacket, feeling a strange powerless anger thrum through him. He recognized the familiarity of it and loathed it so much that he almost pushed her away. But the wobbling of her delicate chin stopped him.

He had barely draped the jacket over her shoulders when she swayed, lost consciousness and folded into his arms like a doll.

Andrea picked her up in his arms with as much gentleness as he was capable of, his heart in his throat. Why had he not listened to her immediately? How had he not seen her pain in her eyes?

His chauffeur helped him lay her on the backseat with her head in his lap. Grabbing a bottle of water, Andrea uncapped it and sprayed a few drops onto her burning forehead, even as he barked orders at Pascale to rush them to the company-owned flat close to the financial district.

He held her head in his lap, arranging her long, bare legs to stretch out onto the seat, and softly tapped her cheek. She didn't respond. His fear grew in his throat, choking him out of air. If anything happened to her because of his arrogance… *Cristo*, he would not forgive himself!

Having drenched a napkin in ice-cold water that was now puddling at his feet, Andrea ran it over her forehead. Slowly, her eyelids fluttered open and she made a half-hearted attempt to sit up. Her hands scrabbled for purchase on his shirt, her lithe softness pressed against him.

He helped her recline against his side, making sure not to touch her back, and held a bottle to her lips.

She drank it down eagerly, coughing and sputtering water until he had to drag the bottle away from her mouth. With a soft gasp, she grabbed the bottle from his hands and poured it over her back and front, dumping cold water all over his leather seats.

"Better?" he asked, as he fished his cell phone out of the jacket that was draped over her shoulders.

"Much, thank you," she said, bare shoulders trembling, whether with the fever he could clearly see in her eyes or with cold, he didn't know. "If you can have Pascale drop me off at—"

"You're not going anywhere alone. You need to be looked after."

"That's not your decision." She licked her chapped lips and softened her tone. "Please, Mr. Valentini. I would prefer—"

"What? No more *Andrea*?" he said, just as the call he'd made on his phone connected.

He wondered what her answer would have been while he barked orders on the phone.

She would not like his high-handedness come tomorrow. She would actively loathe his thoughtfulness and care and generosity tomorrow. But he didn't give a fig.

What did concern him was the couple of cell phones he'd seen focused on him and Monica when he'd been busy cutting the damned dress off her and when he'd carried her to his car. Any other time, he would never have left himself vulnerable to being recorded in a public setting. But the state of her... It was done.

And whatever the consequences, he'd have to deal with them.

Monica had barely discarded his jacket and was holding the bedsheet around her front without it touching the rash when Mr. Valentini returned from his brother Romeo's bathroom with a tube of aloe vera gel that she had told him where to find. Numerous peeks over her shoulder had been unsuccessful for her to get a good look at her back.

With each passing moment, she was aware of what a nuisance this situation was for a man who abhorred any kind of drama or mess, professional or personal. What a nuisance she herself had become for him today.

The last straw in her miserable day had been to find that he had brought her to the apartment he used in the city.

His younger brother, Romeo, had taken one look at her—holding his brother's jacket against her near-naked body—and opened his arms wide to her from his wheel-chair. Monica had thrown herself into his arms shame-lessly, nearly crashing them both to the floor, and sobbed her heart out while he whispered soft endearments into her ear and cursed Francesco to hell and beyond.

The kindness in her friend's eyes had broken through whatever fake armor she'd put on around his brother, making today's loss unbearably real.

Now, with Romeo busy with his physiotherapist, Monica wished she hadn't let go so…completely of her emotions. At least, not where Andrea's frosty gray eyes watched her and judged her and found her so…*pathetic*.

That was the word he had used for her. She couldn't let herself forget it. Not because the ruthless Andrea Val-entini had pronounced it so, but because it was what her foolish desperation for love had reduced her to.

Now, looking up at Andrea as he prowled toward the bed, toward her, Monica tried not to be caught up in the indescribable masculine energy of the man. It had been so from the first moment she'd met him four years ago. Even then, it had been her on the hospital bed and him glaring down at her with those inscrutable gray eyes, making her skin prickle with awareness, even amidst the happy haze of painkillers. As if he blamed her for his mother's mugging incident, rather than thanking her for saving her life.

Nearly three years of close proximity hadn't dimmed his frightful appeal one bit. Proving her efficiency and efficacy to him and the company hadn't stopped her in-sides from tying into knots every time he stepped close. Understanding his work ethic and his care for his em-ployees and his utter intolerance for incompetence and greed hadn't helped conquer this...ridiculous attack of nerves whenever she was near him.

He's just a man, she told herself, like she always did. Made of flesh and bones and hand-stitched designer suits. *But what a man*, the same voice whispered, the bold, brave one she never let out.

With his jacket gone, his cuffs rolled back to reveal hair-roughened corded forearms, the front of his shirt damp and wrinkled thanks to her, he looked less like the suave, sophisticated, steely-eyed businessman and more like...the big, bad boss of a nefarious enterprise. Even his hair, always slickly pushed back, looked as if he'd run his hands through it multiple times, and his mouth had the pinched look that conveyed strain he rarely let rise to the surface.

His meeting with his ex and her father...

Monica's gaze slipped to his left hand, looking for the ring she'd been expecting for weeks now.

"What are you looking for?" he said, leaning one knee onto the bed while she instantly scuttled back like a frightened cockroach.

His mouth flattened at her reaction.

Her cheeks heated, and she hoped he would just put it down to the feverish haze that still racked her body. "I wondered if I should offer congratulations," she said, feeling a boldness she'd never known before. Maybe this moment of bravery came with him having seen her at her worst already. Maybe this was the illusion of wisdom since she'd paid dearly for her naive foolishness.

"Congratulations?" he asked, frowning.

"On your engagement to Mrs. Rossi."

"How the hell did you know that her father was going

to demand that as a condition to the merger?" he said, a sudden coldness to his gaze.

She shivered, his anger a freezing blast against her overheated skin. "We ran into her at dinner one evening, almost six weeks ago. Even before your mother invited her, she joined us."

"Ran into whom?"

"Chiara Rossi," Monica said and sighed. "Flora told me she's Mr. Brunetti's daughter. She was very warm toward your mother. When Flora introduced me as your assistant, gushing how invaluable you find me and couldn't do without me and that I was almost a Valentini family member—" Monica blushed as he watched her with that relentless gaze, though he didn't deny his mother's claims "—it was like a switch had flipped. She kept probing about our working relationship and…" She bit her lip. "When Flora went to the restroom, Mrs. Rossi asked really pointed questions about how well I know you and how much time I spend with you and other intrusive stuff that made me very uncomfortable."

"You could have refused to answer her."

Monica stared at him. "She's your…friend," she said, instead of "apparently the lost love of your life", "and I…didn't want to give offense." She blew out a breath at having gotten that much out.

"You're not answerable to anyone other than me, Ms. D'Souza," he said, running a hand through his hair. "What else?" he asked, his gaze taking in every nuance of hers.

"At the end, she said to make sure I had my head screwed on straight around you, to not lose myself in silly, girlish dreams. To remember that I was nothing but your employee. And then she…"

"What, Monica?"

"She muttered something in Italian, obviously assuming I wouldn't understand."

"What?"

"That she would make sure my time with you was limited, beginning right then."

"You didn't think to warn me of this?"

"Warn you?" Monica said, frustration creeping into her tone. "Of what? That a stunning, sophisticated woman, your ex, apparently a…member of your family's intimate circle, interrogated me about…us? You would have thrown me out of your office before I could get started on that story, calling it gossip. And even if you did hear me out, I didn't know if you would trust my version."

"When have I ever given you the belief that I don't trust you? *Dio mio*, give yourself some credit," he said through gritted teeth. "I could have walked into that meeting with Brunetti without being blindsided by his ultimatum."

"You've been out with her to the opera and that charity gala the last few months. Spent time with her more than I've ever known you to, with any woman, in four years. I thought it was a foregone conclusion. Flora said mergers and marriages were interchangeable in high society."

"You didn't even want to know if her threat had credibility with me? About your position?"

Monica sighed, wondering if he really didn't see. "Pit myself against a woman who knew you for years, who was about to marry you, who has power and prestige and wealth and ask you to pick her or me?"

"You continue to sell yourself short and that is a pathetic trait," he said, shoving away from the bed.

She flinched, feeling his disappointment worse than the sudden crack in his temper. Still, she couldn't stop herself from asking, "So it is not…a done deal?"

Turning, he glared at her.

"I'm not fishing for gossip. I'm merely asking, especially since I've pulled you away from a meeting with her father. I know how much you've sunk into the merger and how many livelihoods depend on it, and how hard you've worked on this. If—"

"Your little drama today hasn't affected the merger. Now drop it. When you need to know anything more, you will."

Monica bristled at his dismissal, though she should be used to it. On one hand, he told her to value herself when it came to him and on the other…he shut her down. Not that she didn't understand his frustration.

Mr. Valentini thrived on being in control, and Carlo Brunetti's addendum must have come as a shock.

While he had shut her line of questioning down, it was clear that he wasn't dating his ex, wasn't the least bit interested in getting back with her or marrying her. Suddenly, it felt like a weight she hadn't known she was carrying had been lifted from her shoulders.

And then, in that feverish haze, it dawned on her that even Francesco abandoning her had less weight in the face of her boss's continued single state. Pressing her hand to her forehead, Monica shivered anew.

Had she been so shaken by Mrs. Rossi's threat that

she'd soon cut Monica out of Andrea's life that she had thrown herself into seeking security with Francesco? For nearly three years, her boss had been the locus of her life, the sole foundation to the kind of security she'd always craved. Andrea's needs and demands and requirements of her had become her sole focus, her reason to get through the day.

Had she so feared losing what little she had of Andrea that she had taken such a reckless, uncharacteristic move and thrown her lot in with Francesco? Had she made him into something he'd never been because she'd worried she was losing her place in Andrea's life?

How bad was her fixation with Andrea Valentini? How had she not seen it?

She was shaking over this new realization when Andrea reached her and opened his palm to reveal two painkillers. "I've spoken to Mama's doctor. He will visit you before nightfall. In the meantime, he suggested these for that fever. He will do blood tests to make sure no lasting damage was done."

"I'm sure it wasn't," she said, wanting not to discuss this with him anymore. Needing this torment to be over. "It's not late. You could just send Pascale to drop me off at the doctor's. That way—"

"And then have Mama castigate me that she didn't raise me to be such a thoughtless, uncaring brute? Save me from a lecture, an extra trip and the headache of an argument with you now, Ms. D'Souza."

CHAPTER THREE

APPARENTLY, ABUNDANCE WAS the name of the game today when it came to Mr. Valentini's choice words for her.

Monica tried to take the pills out of his hand without touching him unnecessarily, resulting in the two red pills dancing off his palm onto the bed. With a curse, he flushed them out, picked up the glass of water and said, "Open."

Feeling like a child who'd gotten in more trouble while actively trying to avoid it—the story of her life— Monica swallowed the protest at his manner and opened her mouth. The faster she could get him out of here, the better she could wallow in her misery.

But it was impossible to follow her head's warnings when his fingers gripped her chin in a firm grasp and her nostrils were full of that dark clove-and-pine scent of his, and the corded column of his throat and his angular chin and that thin slash of his mouth filled her hazy gaze. And then there was the scar that ran from his temple to the side of his mouth, somehow adding to his appeal as a grumpy beast of a man.

Monica shivered again and it had nothing to do with whatever fever the chemicals from the dress had induced in her.

He noticed that, too. "The doctor said the aloe was a good idea until he can give you a stronger steroid. He recommended we air out your skin as much as possible. So, lie down so that I can—"

"That's not necessary at all," Monica said, trembling from head to toe now at the thought of his fingers on her bare flesh.

And there was the second part of the thing she'd missed.

There was a reason she'd always avoided anything even remotely nearing forced intimacy with Mr. Valentini—not even risking a nightcap in the confines of his office after thirteen hours of constant negotiations resulting in a deal last year; not a ride in his car after a long day to the apartment she shared with four other women—and she was becoming aware of the why of it only now.

Shame burned through her chest, adding to all the other burns currently attacking her tender flesh and battered heart. Had she convinced herself that Francesco was it for her because of how out of control her life felt with her boss's alleged upcoming engagement? How long had she been attracted to him without even being aware of it?

It took Mr. Valentini's hand on her wrist to realize she'd started crawling away from him, the sheets now tangled around her legs. The frost of his gray eyes should have been enough to cool down her burning flesh in an instant. "There's no one else to tend to you here and I would rather not move you tonight. If you prefer Romeo to me, I can call him. Only then he'll insist on missing his physiotherapy session and remain here with you. Your choice."

"That's not a choice at all," Monica whispered in a small voice, knowing that she was making it worse by stretching this out. For both of them.

"Lie down," he said in that firm voice, and her body automatically began to obey him. "It's nothing I've not seen before, Ms. D'Souza. And maybe this will teach you to not act so prideful when Mama offers you a present once in a while."

Halfway through her turn, Monica straightened and glared at him. "I can't accept monetary gifts from Flora any more than I can accept them from you."

"I've not offered you any," he said, something flickering in his gaze.

Monica wondered how she wasn't going up in smoke at all the embarrassment she was causing herself. "I know that. And I wasn't hinting that you should," she said, feeling more and more flustered by the second. "I'm just saying it would be the—"

"Please, continue…enlightening me about how your mind works."

"I know what you think of Romeo's friends who come to him for his clout and his wealth. I know what you think of your cousins who are forever asking you or Flora for handouts. I know how easily people fall in your esteem and how ruthlessly you cut them out of—"

"I did not realize you held my opinion in such esteem," he said, frowning. "*Dio mio*, why would I count you as one of those leeches if you accept a frivolous dress or a handbag from Mama? What's the big risk if you accept it?" His frown morphed into a thunderous scowl. "You're afraid I will take your job away? You should trust in—"

"What? Of course not. You would never do anything

so unethical. I just…" She hesitated, feeling as if she was baring herself to him on more than one level. "Please, just forget it."

She was about to turn around when he arrested her once again. This time, his fingers spanned more of her flesh, her shoulder to be specific. Her bare shoulder.

Monica could feel the ridged abrasions of each of his fingers like a divot on her flesh. As if the mere touch was stamping her *Property of Andrea Valentini*. And the worst thing was that she didn't even mind the feverish jumps her imagination was taking. What the hell was wrong with her?

Her attempt to stop jerking away made her do a weird convulsion on the bed, pulling her closer to his hard body. She wiped at her damp lip and wondered what she'd done wrong in this life to receive such torment. "You trust me in a professional setting, then?"

"Of course, I do. In a personal setting, too. Because you operate it with the same principles."

He pulled back as if he needed a wider view of her, and his mouth—why was she looking at his mouth constantly?—lost that annoyed set. "Then what is it you fear would happen if you accepted Mama's gifts? If say, you had let her buy you a nice wedding dress instead of this chemical-soaked death trap that has caused you so much pain? If you had let her meet Francesco a few times and make sure he was right for you?"

Monica blinked back a new spurt of tears. When he put it like that, when she thought this all could have been avoided, she truly felt pathetic. "I have gotten so used to all the time I spend with Flora and Romeo. I like having them in my life. I adore meeting her for dinner every Wednesday. I adore playing chess with Romeo and practicing Italian with him and just…being around him. I have never had such wonderful people who…cared about me in my life before. I don't want to do a single thing that would jeopardize that."

"And my second question?"

"I…" Monica met his gaze and then skittered away. Clearly, he wasn't going to let go until she admitted what a fool she'd been. "Francesco was desperate to meet Flora. And Romeo. And you. Especially after I confessed how sweet it was that Flora wanted to buy me jewelry for the wedding. Then there was that one time when you picked me up in the middle of our date and demanded that I find that communication with the Japanese company… He was elated that whole day. I think because he realized how much you valued my work."

In retrospect now, Monica could see that Francesco had proposed soon after that. He'd also been unbelievably annoyed until she agreed to bring him to the Valentini estate sometime to meet them all. "Something about his eagerness didn't…sit well with me."

"And yet you chose to bury that instinct?" Mr. Valentini sounded so angry that Monica felt herself shrink under his gaze. But enough was enough. She'd already let one man treat her like garbage.

She looked up, meeting that gray gaze straight on. "He is an orphan, like me. Wanting shiny things like a new car or nice clothes or wanting to use my connection to you to establish himself in his life is not wrong, Mr. Valentini. Not all of us are born into wealth *and* a loving family."

A curse escaped his mouth, the contempt in his eyes

deepening. Monica swallowed at the intense reaction, fighting the need to fix it.

"So you think he was right to use you like he did?"

"Not if he loved me a little and thought it was an advantage we could use to build our future. Not when I've worked hard to build that reputation with you. Not when life is…hard and unfair. But he didn't love me at all and he thought I was a foolish girl with outdated ideas. He's made that clear."

His rough fingers lifting her chin sent Monica's pulse skittering across her body like an unearthed wire. If she'd expected to see tenderness in his eyes, she'd have been disappointed. "Whatever you do or don't do in the future, it would be impossible to separate Mama and Romeo from you, Ms. D'Souza. Even if I wished it. Neither of them will stand for it. Trust me in that, too, *si*?"

"Si," she said, trying to not drown in the warmth that promise drenched through her.

"Once your fever goes down, you're moving to the estate while you recover." He pressed a finger to her parted lips before she could protest. "Let Mama look after you. Spend more time with Romeo. He's always complaining that I work you too hard. *Si*?"

"Si."

"Mama thinks of you as her daughter and wants to spoil you, just a little. With me and Romeo, she does not have a chance to indulge that side of her. So next time, when she begs to buy you a little something, just for her own pleasure, let her, *si*?"

Monica licked her dry lips. If he asked her in that tone, she was afraid she'd agree to anything. *"Si."*

Something hot and feral sparked in his eyes and was shut down before she could even be sure she'd seen it.

Andrea Valentini was not attracted to her, no. Not at all. Never in a million years. He was too old and experienced and sophisticated and cynical and gorgeous and way too out of her silly, safe, secure sphere to *like her* like that. God, she couldn't even say it right in her own head.

This wasn't a relationship she would ever mess up by forcing her own stupid romantic ideals on it. Never. Her fever was clearly making her hallucinate.

"Now, lie down and let me finish this."

"Si," she said automatically and plopped, facedown, onto the bed.

There were two different fevers going on in her body, she thought with a near hysterical giggle trapped in her throat. One was caused by the rash on her back, and the other made her nipples pinch deliciously against the cool sheets, her entire body thrumming in anticipation of his touch.

His sudden laughter exploded into the space between them, running down her spine like a warm, delicious trickle that was both comforting and arousing. Just the husky, deep sound of it did things to her belly and lower, more effectively than Francesco ever could have. She burrowed her cheek into the cool pillow, grateful that he couldn't see her face right now. The last thing she needed was for her expressive face to give away her...arousal.

"You are dangerous, Ms. D'Souza. A man could get used to hearing all those yeses from such a mouth."

Monica tried to stay stiff, even as his words filled her with a delicious ache.

No, he wasn't flirting with her. Not at all.

"Surprising that you think it might go to your head, Mr. Valentini," she said, fighting the urge to catch his gray gaze, "when you're unused to hearing anything but yes from the whole world."

"You're not as malleable and lacking in spine as you think you are," he said gruffly, after a beat of silence that crackled with tension. "I definitely do not remember you blindly agreeing to anything I proposed. In fact, your meteoric rise through the company to my side has to do with how well you stand up to me, even as you act like a scurrying mouse."

Monica blinked back the surge of grateful tears and wriggled against the sheets, feeling an ache between her thighs. "Mouse, huh? That's the nicest thing you've ever said to me." Feverish or not, those words of affirmation out of Mr. Valentini's mouth made pleasure skitter through her. "Maybe what I have is a praise kink and not this crazy attraction to him," she said into the pillow, not realizing she'd spoken aloud until it was too late.

Behind her, she could feel Andrea still.

God, please, don't let him have heard.

"I'm ready," she said loudly, desperate to get this over with.

She stayed stiff and unmoving when the cool, soothing gel landed on her back.

She somehow kept her breath steady as his fingers spread the cold gel over the rash, skating nearly to her buttocks and upward, his touch incredibly gentle, as if he was an experienced skier in full control of his path.

When his fingers moved up and around to spread the gel to her side boob and to the back of her neck, and when the bed shifted and groaned under her when he leaned forward to reach her other side, and when she felt his breath on her back and his scent filled her nostrils, Monica could do nothing about the dampness that bloomed between her thighs. Or the sudden, painfully alive ache that pulsed at her core.

So much for Francesco calling her prudish and unresponsive. His touch, his kisses, just hadn't done it for her, because he wasn't the one she really wanted.

Especially when she'd spent most of her life trying to downplay her body, dressing in frumpy clothes, wary of attracting the wrong kind of men. In the end, she'd started believing that she wasn't much of a sexual creature to begin with. At twenty-three, she'd never felt the need to try sex. Even with her fiancée, she hadn't been eager.

And yet, apparently, all her boss had to do was breathe in her direction and she was ready to go up in flames. It was knowledge she could have done without.

For the first time that miserable day, she cursed Francesco for putting her in this position, even though she was beginning to understand that he wasn't really to blame. For proposing to her. For making her buy this shitty dress. For making it all gray and confusing and yet...*deliciously right*. For putting her in a situation where she knew without a doubt that Mr. Valentini's touch made her shiver, always had, because she was unbelievably attracted to him.

She was attracted to her ruthless, grumpy boss, and if she so much as betrayed the fact, it didn't bode well for her future with his company, or with his family.

* * *

Andrea had never been in this place where desire thrummed through his veins in a sluggish beat, slowing down the world itself around him. The only time that came remotely close had been when he'd tried a cannabis brownie with Romeo because his brother's pain had been unbearable and he hadn't wanted to do it alone.

Never again, Andrea had promised himself when all it had done was intensify his feelings around the loss of his father.

Not even as a twenty-year-old who'd been deep in the throes of lust with Chiara and had been determined to win her at any cost, had he felt this delicious heaviness in his limbs.

Now, as he covered his assistant's bottom with a sheet and applied the goopy gel to her back, it felt like he was charting the dips and valleys of her smooth, golden-brown skin. As if he was compiling a database of how she reacted to what kind of touch.

Her soft groans of relief shouldn't tighten his own muscles so much that he wanted to send his fingers on further exploration of her unmarred skin, of the tight cinch of her waist, of the swell of her hips...until she knew his touch everywhere. And it wasn't just the physical hunger he felt for her.

It was an inexplicable, overwhelmingly possessive urge to fix all the wrongs that had been done to Ms. D'Souza, to give her everything she'd ever dreamed of in her life.

Cristo, the woman's back was red and angry and she was literally in pain, on top of the humiliation she'd endured today. And still, some invisible spark she'd set off banged against the outer shell Andrea had covered himself in over the years.

It was her vulnerability—as raw and visceral as the rash on her back. He found it…tasteless, and yet it clung to him, making him wish he could pull something over to cover them both from his sight.

Maybe because it reminded him of how he'd once felt. How the accident had left him raw and aching with loss and fear. He never wanted to be at the mercy of such fear again.

And truly, something had been cauterized in him with his father's death. He had gone from a wild, incessant partygoer who cared about nothing but soccer and women to a responsible businessman whose duty was to his family overnight. But something more had been lost, too.

And he didn't regret that loss just as he didn't regret the loss of that wild lifestyle. Only that his father had never had a chance to see how responsible and capable Andrea could be, that he had died terrified for Romeo and for his family.

Ms. D'Souza's face when she'd revealed how important his mother and brother were to her and how she never wanted to lose them…that kind of attachment would only set her up for pain and disappointment and loss. And yet, he had made the foolish promise that she would not lose them.

He jumped off the bed, wiping his hands on the end of a sheet. He needed to get out of here and figure a way out of Chiara's father's ridiculous ultimatum. He hated being manipulated like she and her father were doing. Didn't like being pushed into a corner.

And now there was this...headache, in the form of this innocent, naive creature lying down in front of him. With whom he spent more time than he did anyone else in a given week. The last thing he needed was this attraction messing up a perfect professional relationship. If it was simply lust, he wouldn't give a damn about it. But he had a feeling it wasn't.

It was...more. Even admitting that stuck in his craw, but he wasn't a man who thrived on delusions. He'd rather face the problem and fix it than drape himself in lies.

"When you come back, we'll find you a position with a different department. Maybe you can go back to the CFO. Maria has been bitterly vocal that I stole you from her."

Her silence told him he had hurt her. But Andrea couldn't afford to care. She needed toughening up to begin with and she had failed in not communicating to him that Chiara had acted like they were already married. Her usefulness had been defeated by this...inconvenient attraction, on his part, and her awe of him.

"It will be the same designation and pay," he added, wanting to clarify that he wasn't punishing her.

After tense moments of silence, she shifted a little on the bed, clutching onto the sheet as if it were a lifejacket, and hissed out a pained breath before she faced him.

Her eyelids were swollen, and the tip of her nose was flushed pink. Sweat made silky tendrils of hair stick to her forehead and she dug her teeth into her lower lip, making it glisten a dark pink.

But it was the expression in her eyes that caught him.

There was so much there, too much that he didn't want to see. She released her lip and sighed. "That's for the best. Although—" a small smile blossomed "—you might have to tone it down a bit if you want to keep an assistant. Not everyone is as…"

"Brave as you are?" He raised a brow.

"I was going to say *efficient*."

"So you're not upset about it," he said, wanting to poke and prod a little. *Dio mio*, why was he being so contrary?

She shrugged and the sheet slipped a bit to reveal the curve of a plump breast. Andrea had to look away, though he couldn't ignore the jolt of lust tightening through him. "You've never hidden how much you loathe the personal crossing over into the professional. Flora's…fondness for me would have put us at odds sooner or later. This way, at least I haven't…" She trailed off.

"Haven't what, Monica?" he said, insulted and injured, like a young cub trying to prove himself. Apparently, working for him had less hold for her than her attachment to his mother.

"Made a fool of myself."

"What do you…" His curiosity disappeared when his gaze landed on the scar that was the length of his hand span on her waist. The scar she'd acquired when she'd saved his mother.

Andrea felt as if he was suddenly drenched in a cold bucket of water. He could have lost his mother if not for this foolish, brave woman's rash actions. *Cristo*, she hadn't even been a woman but a mere girl of nineteen, jumping to a stranger's rescue. And in return, she'd gotten a blade to her belly, nearly cleaving her waist in two.

A rush of shame swamped him. How had he not made

it a point to learn how badly she had been hurt? How had he just shrugged off her injury as if it was a minor inconvenience, a small price to pay for his mother's safety? How had he thought her unwillingness to accept cash in return an irritability?

"Turn to the side," he said, unable to even modulate his tone toward a request.

"What? Is it the sheets? I will wash them and make sure—"

"Forget about the damned sheets. Turn to the side, Monica," he repeated, his strides eating up the distance to the bed.

Slowly, looking like a frightened rabbit, tugging the sheet higher between her breasts, she followed his command.

He couldn't help it, even if he tried. And he didn't try that hard to stop himself.

He rubbed a finger over the scar that inched from front to back on her right side, at the tight, tiny juncture of her waist, as wide as the span of three of his fingers together and reaching back.

The gash must have been deep to leave such a scar, despite the fact that Mama had had her transferred to the best doctors immediately. All he had cared about was that his mother was unharmed.

"I didn't realize you were hurt this badly," he said, in a thin voice that shivered with anger and fear that felt as fresh as it had when he'd first learned of the mugging incident. And yet, the source was different. The source of those thorny emotions was new.

"I don't even remember that it's there anymore," she replied in a muffled voice, and he realized the painkillers had finally kicked in. "Sometimes, though, when I leave work after dark, and you know that street behind the bus depot, I get a flash of like…fear. And you know the weirdest thing? The scar burns then. I know it sounds ridiculous because as you can see, it's all healed but—"

"Just because the burn is not real doesn't mean you don't feel it."

She sighed, her body trembling and then settling. "Francesco said I was being a scaredy-cat."

"Do me a favor, Ms. D' Souza. Stop telling me about all the foolish, idiotic things that man led you to believe."

"I think that's a fair ask," she said.

"If you would like, I'll take you to see a specialist. We can get rid of the scar," he said, running his finger again over the thick pink-white scar tissue. "It mars your beauty."

She laughed into the pillow, the sound half-muffled and half-airy, as if she couldn't get enough breath into her lungs. "My so-called beauty has never done me any favors. And honestly, I don't care about the scar. I'm only glad Flora remained unhurt that awful day."

Andrea ran his hand one last time over the scar, knowing that he was crossing a line she and he had both clearly demarcated between them. But the damned thing was that he wanted to touch the scar again. He wanted to press his mouth to it, lick it, take away whatever phantom pain it had left behind and make it mean something else for her. Make it a source of pleasure.

He wanted to lie down beside her and turn her to face him, until her breathtaking features lit upon him. Until she bared herself to him willingly, until she stretched into his touch. Until she begged him to explore this…prickly heat between them. Until she of the generous smiles and the gushing compliments and brave little heart was all his to do with as he wanted.

Oh, how he would play with her and tease her and taunt her until that shyness faded and she came to him, ready and brave, willing putty in his hands.

He jumped off the bed as though he was the one scalded, as though it was his back that was on fire.

Cristo, she was twenty-three and naive and not for him. *In any way.* Not even for a single night, he told himself, crushing the wicked whisper of desire.

"Andrea?" she whispered when he was almost at the door.

He turned to find her watching him, a sudden alertness to her drowsy gaze. *"Si?"*

"Can I ask you something?"

"Si."

"Are you angry with me?"

"Yes," he said, letting his irritation flare. "You know how much I don't like unnecessary headaches in my life. I know way too much about you that I didn't need to."

"I won't fight the transfer but you...you won't let this change—"

"Si, Monica. Now, sleep."

She giggled then and it made him still. When he looked back, *one more time*, her eyes were closed, the thick, long lashes casting crescents onto her cheeks in the shadows as he closed the automatic blinds. Her nostrils flared, and a small secretive little smile split her mouth. "You also said yes three times. A girl could get used to that. A girl could feel heady with the power of hearing so many yeses from *Andrea Valentini*. Any girl. Even silly, stupid, pathetic me."

Then she snored and drifted off to sleep and Andrea knew he had to stay away from her. Completely.

Before the little good sense that was left in him was consumed by raw want. Before he gave in and did something his father would have been appalled by. Before this inappropriate lust for a woman under his protection turned into something more dangerous that would only end in hurting her.

CHAPTER FOUR

IN THE FIRST two weeks that Monica was at Flora Valentini's house—their family home in a postcard-like village near Lake Como—Andrea hadn't come to see her once.

No, not to see her, but to visit with his mother, Monica modified in her head. The fact that in two weeks, Andrea hadn't visited Flora and Romeo once *was* kind of alarming.

If there was one thing she knew about him for sure, it was that he was devoted to his mother and brother.

Was it because she was here? Because after all the drama she'd inadvertently started, he couldn't stand to see her pathetic face?

Monica had resisted the idea of staying at his home—his high-handed order—for the first two days. But under Flora's gentle care and with Romeo's cheerful company, she had decided not to fight one of the few favors life had handed her. It wasn't like she caused an imposition to either of them.

Flora was exactly the kind of mother she'd have chosen in any universe, if she was given the chance. And learning that the older woman thought of her as a daughter was a gift Andrea had given her. The one gift she didn't resent, when she was already buried under obligation for all the favors he'd done her.

Monica had cried a lot the first two weeks. Some of it had been tears of pain and relief because the doctor had told her that Andrea's immediate intervention and having seen her the very day she had collapsed had staved off infection and scarring. Some of her tears had been for this new consuming awareness of a man who was so out of her sphere. To think she'd nearly married a man she didn't even love just to escape the pain of being thrown out of his life…

But she also reminded herself that, if not for Flora, Mr. Valentini would have no interest in her personal life. He wouldn't have noticed if she had dropped dead that day at those steps. Until she was absent from his life and it fell apart without her brisk efficiency, Andrea Valentini wouldn't have taken note of her absence any more than he'd taken note of her presence over four years.

So yes, while she'd recovered and screwed her head on straight under Flora's gentle care, she wasn't going to read anything into the sudden flare of heat that had arced between them that afternoon. Any woman would feel discombobulated when seeing a man like him—gorgeous and smoldering—attend to her personally. And she had already been under such shock and in pain, had been vulnerable and desperate for a small kindness.

The little hope she'd nurtured the beginning of the third week that she could slowly transition out of his life and into her new role with the CFO was blown to bits when Romeo shared the little clip of her and Andrea that had gone viral. Of him cutting through the dress and then carrying her to his car, while she was half-naked and delirious and the accompanying narrative the press had spun around it. If he'd thought her a nuisance before, he probably actively hated her now. When she'd called Mr. Valentini yesterday, she'd been unable to reach him.

Then he arrived suddenly the next evening, like the storm clouds that had suddenly gathered, threatening a downpour. Romeo and she had just finished an invigorating chess game that she had lost, yet again, sitting in the small garden that separated the manicured lawns from the thick orange groves and dense woods beyond.

A prickling at her nape was the thing that intimated Monica of her boss's arrival, as if there was now a chip sewn under her skin, programmed to detect his proximity. She looked up to find him standing on a wide balcony off the second floor, kissing Flora's cheek while the older woman animatedly greeted him. His gray gaze was, however, intensely focused on Monica.

Even across the field separating them, she could see the pinch of his eyebrows because he didn't want his mother to know of his thunderous mood. Unable to hold his gaze any longer, Monica swallowed and looked away. Butterflies took flight in her belly, making it impossible to sit still. Her muscles called for action, either to run toward him or far away, into the woods maybe.

"What was that?" Romeo asked from across the small table, his gaze switching between her and his brother.

"What was what?" Monica asked, trying a fake casualness with all her might.

"That look in your eyes. Monica, are you scared of my brother?" he asked, reaching for her hand across the table.

"What? No," she said, warmth cresting her cheeks. At

Romeo's unconvinced expression, she sighed. "Maybe a little, yes. Especially after this…episode I've caused."

She pulled his hand forward and draped it across her cheek. All her life, she'd been starved for touch. And Romeo was one of those very few men on the planet, in her limited experience of them, who seemed to need it as much as she did, without thinking it somehow decreased his masculinity. When he cupped her cheek, she pressed herself into it. "I'm a coward."

He *tsked* and she looked up. His gray eyes—so much like Andrea's, except tempered with natural kindness and constant pain—gleamed with warmth. "You're the bravest person I know."

She scoffed. "Is it open season on me, then?"

"Or maybe the wisest?" He scrunched his nose. "Very few people on this planet understand my brother's moods."

"Yes, that," she said, jumping on the lifeline he offered. "I know An— *Mr. Valentini's* moods better than anyone. Right now, you might imagine he's simply listening to your mother talk a mile a minute at him, but he's in a foul mood. And obviously, it's to do with me."

Romeo looked at his brother and then back at her. "Perhaps, but not in the way you imagine, *cara.*"

"You're just having fun at my expense, you scoundrel."

He picked up her hand and kissed the back of it, a sudden unholy glint to his gaze. "You never told me what happened that day, after he brought you home. The fact that my sainted brother hasn't visited in three weeks to check on Mama and me is…shocking. Something must have happened to keep him away so thoroughly."

Monica shrugged, her mouth suddenly dry, her heart

palpitating at a dangerous rate. By the time he'd left, she'd been out of it. Had he made the decision to transfer her because she had said something she shouldn't have? Had she betrayed her stupid attraction? "He took care of my back, told me what a nuisance he considered me, declared he was transferring me to another department and left."

"And yet, you have been helping smooth over things these last two weeks, *si*?"

"Just some knowledge transfer," she said dismissively. But at least, in this, she could feel pride in a job done well. While she had left behind systems to deal with everything he worked on, no other person could come close to understanding him.

"Oh, come, don't downplay your virtues, *bella*. I bet Andrea can't do without you. And that dark scowl he's wearing is because he has realized that, too. If there's one thing I know about my brother, it's that he hates needing anyone."

Her gaze finding Andrea unerringly, Monica mulled over Romeo's insight into her boss. "What about Mrs. Rossi, then?" she asked, before she could curb her tongue. The question had been burning a hole through her for three weeks. Every morning, noon and evening, she expected to see the sophisticated woman walk in and declare that she was Andrea's fiancée and throw her out. Or at least express her satisfaction that he had already moved Monica to a different department. Even though he'd told her the engagement wasn't happening.

She had literally stood in front of a mirror every night and practiced the facial expression she'd put on when she congratulated the happy couple. She was determined not to betray her own tangled thoughts on the matter, nor the belated feelings of righteous resentment that Chiara Rossi had no right to talk to her like she had.

"*Even you* can't believe that Andrea marrying Chiara would have anything to do with needing her. My brother is incapable of the particular emotion you walk around looking for."

"Now you're beginning to sound like him," Monica said, hearing the unspoken ache in Romeo's voice.

She reached for his hand again, her heart aching for this man who had become such a good friend to her in the past four years while his brother had remained a fascinating mystery. And he needed to remain one. While the transfer had hurt, Monica realized now that it was a blessing in disguise. She needed to stay away from Mr. Valentini, far away.

Turning, she focused on her friend. "Now, how about we leave Mr. Valentini to his brooding and you tell me about that waitress who begged for your number at that restaurant last week?"

"What will you do? Andrea?"

Andrea had to tear his gaze away from the scene being enacted out in the garden, no doubt on purpose, by Romeo. A part of him was delighted that in Monica's company, Romeo was rediscovering the fun-loving, outgoing, stunt-per-day rascal that he had been as a teen before the accident had bound him to the wheelchair. Papa had been driving in a dangerous snowstorm, while Andrea had been screaming at him like a thwarted toddler, leading to the accident that had stolen him from them.

Another part of him, the part that he'd unsuccessfully been trying to beat into submission, roared like some low-cognitive-capacity Neanderthal watching his woman being chummy with another man.

His woman... Madre de Dio, where was this uncivilized possessive streak coming from?

Maybe because he hadn't spent a single day since the accident doing one thing for himself, he told himself now, searching for some rational explanation. Those first few years, he'd simply functioned on autopilot, running himself ragged between stopping a hostile takeover and getting Romeo everything he needed, and relieving Mama whenever he could at his brother's side so she could rest and grieve losing the man she had loved.

After that, after they'd learned to live with the gaping hole his father had left behind, after Romeo had made peace with the fact that he might never walk again, Andrea had still continued in the same way.

Even now, as he watched, Romeo pulled Monica into his lap and hummed some melody that Andrea could just barely hear. With one arm thrown around his neck, one clasped in Romeo's, Monica was laughing.

He could hear that inelegant snort that came at the end of her laugh, see the way her whole body shook, and he could just imagine how she would smell of sun and vanilla, a strange, erotic scent he associated with her now.

With his other hand, Romeo was wheeling the chair forward and backward, moving their clasped hands. When Monica bent down to kiss his cheek, her long dark hair fell forward like a curtain, covering them both in whisper-thin darkness. As if to taunt him.

"Andrea? What will you do about—"

"Is he more than fond of her? Romeo?" he asked, suddenly remembering the frantic call Romeo had made, right after Mama had, demanding that Andrea do something about Francesco and the sudden wedding.

Andrea had known they were both fond of her, but this possibility… A sick feeling twisted in his stomach. If his brother really *liked* Monica, when Andrea had just discovered such deep… It didn't bear thinking. Out of the miasma of confusion, a selfish, primal, competitive want roared.

"Of Monica?" Mama said, an instant smile teasing her mouth. "Wouldn't it be wonderful if he were? She is such a lovely girl, Andrea, and she does make him laugh like before…the accident and that business with that girl." His mother pursed her mouth and sighed. "I know Monica might be open to trying something but I also know it is not fair to her. His heart and mind are not yet in a good place."

Andrea grunted. Everyone she came across, at work or in personal life, whether it lasted a day or a week or a moment, Monica seemed to win them over. He found it both infuriating and fascinating. "She just got dumped at city hall at the last minute, Mama. How are you so confident that she would welcome Romeo's advances—" he had to inhale with a conscious effort "—whatever they might be?"

"All Monica wants is family and security and to belong somewhere, and she fits so well already into our family and we all like her, even you, and…"

Whatever she saw in his face, her words trailed off.

Andrea turned just in time to see her gaze widen, her mouth fall open with a soft gasp. As if she'd just seen a tiger setting its target on a doe.

Cristo, he was a thirty-four-year-old man. The last thing he needed was his mother to know he lusted after his very capable, very young, assistant and that it had him thrashing around like a randy teenager. Or that he wanted to act on it, forgetting all his own personal ethics. "Mama, do not—"

"She's too…young, Andrea. And so pure at heart," she finally said, a thread of outrage in her tone.

He laughed and pulled her close, loving her a little more for being so protective of the stranger in their midst. Though he wasn't at all surprised. The Valentini name had always stood for ethics and sound business morals, and his father had made loyalty the highest badge of honor. His mother's warning only reminded him of his father and all the values he had tried to instill in him and Romeo, beginning with the fact that power and privilege shackled a man as much as they liberated him.

"And now this…media scandal about that video…" his mother said, bringing him back to the present. "I demand to know what your plan is."

"I have no plan, Mama. This has already blown up beyond my control."

"So marry Chiara, bring Monica back to work for you and all this…speculation is over. You wanted a future with her once, Andrea." She turned completely and studied him. Her voice softened as she cradled his cheek. Andrea marveled at how little she did that with him these days. All her softness and her maternal instincts were limited to Romeo. *And Monica*, he thought, without an ounce of rancor. "Chiara is sophisticated and smart and she will make you a good wife."

"I am not the same man I was ten years ago."

"Then it is good that she has matured, too, no?"

"It doesn't look like that, given she's letting her father trot her out like some show horse, attached to this merger. If there's one thing I know, it is that Chiara wants power and prestige more than anything. I have nothing against her wishes for her life. But I will not play her games."

His mother looked alarmed, as if she couldn't imagine so much scheming. The simple soul she was, he wasn't surprised. Still, she persisted, taking his hand in hers. "Is it simply wounded pride that she picked a different man over you a decade ago that drives you to say no now?"

"Pride has nothing to do with it. And believe me, I'm grateful that she didn't accept my proposal then. Because now, I'm not that young, prideful buck who needed to prove himself by gaining the biggest prize around. Now, she or marriage…have very little appeal to me."

It was both relieving and sad that his mother did not push him harder toward matrimony or hold the Valentini legacy over his head like some hanging sword. Maybe because she knew where his opposition came from. She had once known the real thing and the loss of it had nearly shattered them all. Once you were witness to something as holy and real as his parents' marriage had been, it felt like blasphemy to enter one that was nothing but a mocking illusion of it. Neither did he think he was made for the real thing, even if it was available to him.

He had lived through enough pain such love wrought on one.

"She and her father are playing a dirty game, threatening to pull back from the merger at this critical point when so many livelihoods depend on its success. They need to learn that I will not bow."

"So you will use Monica?"

"Use her? She's not a doll, Mama, to arrange wherever you or I please. This situation was not of my making and if I twist it to my own advantage, it will be because there is no other choice left. I have my reputation and Valentini's to protect."

Before his mother could further lecture him, Andrea turned around toward the stairs. He had tried to stay away. He'd already had her moved to a different department, though that had only seemed to blow up in his face because Monica was the linchpin for so many matters that came through to him.

But the video circulating on the internet and the story that the media had already woven around it besmirched the Valentini name. The very name his father had given a new meaning to. Andrea could not let it continue. So he would take care of two birds with one shot.

CHAPTER FIVE

ONE LOOK. ONE EXCHANGE between him and Romeo in which Andrea tried to keep his expression vacant—not completely successfully—was enough to know his brother's heart. Conversely, Andrea had no doubt that Romeo now knew what was in his heart, too. Or to be precise, what was swimming like lazy wine in his blood a lot farther south of his heart.

"I was just asking Monica if she is the reason you have neglected us for three weeks," Romeo said, grinning. "Quite the precedent you're setting, Andrea."

Standing by his brother, her gaze landing on and quickly skidding away from Andrea's face, Monica looked like she wanted to run.

"I could be a gentleman like you," Andrea said, unable to stop himself from ruffling Romeo's hair, "and lie, but I'm not. Monica is indeed the reason I couldn't visit. There's a media scandal in the making with her in the middle of it and I have been trying my best to thwart it before it muddies the Valentini name beyond repair."

Monica stiffened and finally, finally, met his gaze. "I called you several times since I found out two days ago, Mr. Valentini. You didn't pick up."

Andrea felt that same lazy thrum again. His gaze traversed her length, greedy, and all-consuming.

In four years, he had never seen her dressed so casually. In denim shorts that showed off her legs that went on forever and a tiny, tight V-neck crop top that bared her shoulders and a strip of her midriff, she looked like the gelato he used to be eager for on a hot summer day. Her hair was tied in a high ponytail, highlighting the angular gauntness of her features.

"I know it looks bad but—"

He finally responded to her. "It's not just that someone recorded the entirety of me undressing you and carrying you to my car or that the short clip has been edited with salacious commentary. Today, some investigative reporter decided to inquire after your well-being at Valentini headquarters and she was told that you'd not only been sent off somewhere no one knew by me, but she's now also saying that I abused my power and then when I got bored, fired you."

Monica pressed her fingers to her mouth. "That's… awful."

"The best version is where they speculate that we've been sleeping with each other for a while and that day, I came to sweep you off your feet at the city hall and that you're now a very satisfied but secretive bride. There are memes being made about me."

"This is my fault," Monica said, rubbing her temple.

"I'm not arguing that point," Andrea said dryly, more than irritated by how she leaned automatically toward Romeo, when he was the one who had actually come to her rescue.

"Andrea!" Romeo said, a quick flash of anger in his

eyes. "You can't blame Monica for this. She was unwell. Where was *your* head?"

"No, Romeo. He's right." She moved toward Andrea like a doe walking into the lion's den, shoulders painfully rigid. "I'll do whatever you need to fix it."

Andrea extended his arm, and she licked her lips, considering it as if it were a snake. "Come. I have a plan in mind."

"Why can't we discuss it here?"

"There is the very real danger of my own family coming after me with pitchforks, if I put one step wrong with you, Ms. D'Souza. I did not think you so much of a coward that you would hide behind them."

"I'm not hiding behind anyone," she said, rushing around Romeo, cheeks red, ponytail flying around, gloriously indignant. "You ordered that I stay here, transferred me to a different department and…don't even answer my calls. You decided I was a headache, a pathetic loser, and shuffled me off."

Andrea stilled, watching the finger she poked into his chest. Hurt and something more flashed in her beautiful eyes. "And if I admit that I had more reasons than your so-called flaws—all your words, by the way—to have you transferred?"

"Did you?"

"Si."

"Oh," she said, color rising to her cheeks. "But you think I can help fix this…mess?"

"Si."

"Fine. Tell me what I need to do."

A surge of desire wrapped its fingers around Andrea's

muscles. "Go wait for me in my suite. I need a moment with my brother."

She nodded, squeezed Romeo's hand one more time and then left.

"Do you know that Mama wishes you were together?" he said to his brother, once Monica was out of earshot.

Romeo's face tightened. "Mama has many wishes, Andrea. Pity we can't make them all true, *si*?"

Feeling as powerless as he did years ago, Andrea shook his head. "Romeo—"

"You're not stealing my chance with her."

"She makes you laugh, like before," Andrea said, repeating his mother's words, knowing the precious truth of them.

"She does. She has reminded me of all the things I'm still capable of. She's been a wonderful friend to have in my life. But neither of us is drawn to the other in that way. In the way you're drawn to her."

"That's not what I want to discuss."

"And yet you interfere in *my* life? Keep track of all the waitresses I hook up with? I'm not some fragile princess whose virginity you've been tasked to protect, Andrea."

Andrea's cheeks crested with guilty heat while his heart jumped with joy that his brother had…*scored*, as tasteless as that sounded. It meant Romeo's heart was also healing.

"While I appreciate the grand sacrifice you were about to make on my behalf," Romeo said dryly, "it is unnecessary."

"Don't be so sure that I would *make the sacrifice*," Andrea said, still feeling the pinch of acute selfishness. "I simply would have said may the best man win."

A flicker of shock passed through his brother's eyes before he scoffed. "Just what Monica would like, no? You and me fighting over her like she was a bone." Then his gaze searched Andrea's, as if it had only now dawned on him what his brother had unwittingly betrayed. "You're thinking at less than your usual capacity if you think Monica will be easy to bend to your...strategies. Mama, like the world, only sees part of her."

"*Cristo*, my own family thinks I'm some kind of... twisted monster, getting ready to prey on the innocent lamb."

Romeo laughed, grooves forming around his mouth. "I understand the bind you're in, even if Mama doesn't. I know you need to take aggressive action. Against the scandal and against Brunetti."

"And?"

"I know the tack you're going to take. Probably the only one available to you. And I know where it will lead."

"Romeo—"

"I have seen the way you looked at her just now, Andrea, when she was laughing in my lap. I will even admit that I once felt what you feel—the selfish want that takes you out at your knees, when you as a Valentini man should be the one in control. The one to whom everything should bend and bow."

"And you're going to warn me off?"

"*Cristo*, no. Mama does you a grave injustice by behaving as if I was the only one who lost something in that accident. Why would I warn my brother against something he desperately wants, something that makes him look like he's gloriously alive for the first time in a decade?"

Andrea thrust a hand through his hair, shaken by his brother's depth of perception. Shaken by how his deepest desire sounded so…stark and all-consuming when put into simple words.

"What of your little friend?"

"My *little friend* has more courage in her pinky finger than the rest of the world. You know the biggest gift she's given me in the last four years, Andrea? She showed me what a glorious, wild, wonderful world is out there and how much I still crave to experience it. She just needs to come to that realization, too. And if something does happen to her once she sets her tremendous will to it—" Romeo's gaze, so much like their father's, pinned Andrea to the spot "—then she has me on her side. But I cannot bubble wrap her, just like you can't do to me."

Andrea bent and kissed his brother's rough cheek, feeling a wellspring of gratitude for the woman who had shown his brother who he could be with the simple, expansive, unconditional gift of her friendship.

"You got all the wisdom from Papa. All I got were his good looks," he said, blinking away the tears that rose to his eyes.

Romeo thumped him on his shoulder, his serrated laughter music to Andrea's ears, and wheeled himself along the path back to the house by Andrea's side. "You're not alone in this either, Andrea. If this merger falls through, I mean."

Andrea nodded, feeling like his world might finally be settling into a new place after being shattered a decade ago. It would never be the same without Papa, but it wasn't as horrible as he had let it get over the past few years.

* * *

It was like entering a treasure vault, if the treasure was the inside of Andrea Valentini's intensely private mind and life. With each step she'd taken up the stairs, Monica felt as if she was embarking on some momentous journey that she could not turn back from.

The odd day or two she'd stayed here in the past, and even the past three weeks, she'd always stayed in the guest suite, close to Flora's own. She'd never even been up here.

His suite on the first floor was a paradise made for solitude, different from his steel-and-chrome office. Here it was all glass and wood, with minimum decor, while sunlight poured in, bathing everything in a warm, golden glow. And yet, the space was also innately masculine, sober and serious like the man himself.

One entire wall was taken up with bookshelves, which on further scrutiny revealed to be on racing cars and other extreme sports as well as some business tomes. There were even a few glittering trophies, but Monica's attention was quickly commandeered by the other wall.

By a large portrait of Andrea and Romeo and their father, Giovanni. His arms around his sons' shoulders, Giovanni was clearly full of pride and joy. Tall and distinguished, he had been a handsome man, like his sons, but the thing that radiated from him was an easy kindness that Monica had found in few people in her life. Even with him gone for so many years—in the same accident that had hurt Romeo's legs, Flora had told her—she could sense the older man's legacy in his sons and in the company ethics Andrea so staunchly upheld. To have known such love as they did… That sweet ache for something she'd never known came back to her chest.

Monica lingered in the cool foyer until Andrea swept past her to the massive desk in the adjoining study. For a moment, she wondered if he'd forgotten that he'd invited her up here. Then, his gaze was potent on her back, like a physical caress.

"You were supposed to recover here. Not lose weight."

The chastisement was the last thing she'd expected. She wrapped her arms around her belly self-consciously, her skin feeling far too tight to hold the sensations quivering through her. If she'd known he would be visiting, she'd have covered herself up from head to toe. "I'm sorry my body doesn't perform automatically to your wishes and desires," she said, shocked at her own daring.

His laughter at her back felt like a reward. "Your spirit seems to have more than recovered." The tiny hairs at the nape of her neck prickled with awareness as his gaze moved over her back, mostly left bare by threads of fabric holding the crop top together. Going without a bra suddenly seemed liked the worst idea she'd ever had.

"No pain anymore?"

"None at all."

"I'm glad."

He was not a man to make pageantry of anything, and yet this felt like that. As if something big was looming on the horizon, something she hadn't foreseen in her wildest dreams. Or nightmares.

She needed to take control of this conversation as much as she needed to take control of her life. Turning around, she blurted the first thing that came to her lips.

"If you're going to fire me to do damage control, Mr. Valentini, I'd rather—"

"Mr. Valentini? And, *Cristo*, I'm not firing you. Where is that faith of yours?" His gray gaze flashed with a thread of…hurt?

No, she was seeing things again, apparently a condition she suffered when it came to only him. "Of course, I have faith in you. But I realize how bad this is."

"So the solution is to get rid of the one person who's innocent and powerless in all this?"

She jerked her chin up, a defense mechanism, hating that that was how he saw her. Though it wasn't far from the hard truth, like the dog with the broken leg Romeo had nursed to health a year ago. "No, it isn't. But I also know that you wouldn't just cast me out on the streets or hide me away like some taint upon your name. I was just thinking of the company and your reputation. I… misspoke out of fear and urgency."

"Monica… Whatever else the future holds…with the company, with this scandal, with us, I need you to understand that I would never abuse my power in any way."

"I know that, Andrea," she said, letting him hear the conviction she held deep in her bones. His name on her lips, this time when she wasn't delirious with pain, landed between them like an invocation. To what, she had no idea. But she didn't scuttle her gaze away from his.

It was the one truth she'd always known, even if she hadn't understood anything else about her reaction to him. But uncertainty about the current problem was another beast. She addressed the thing that was bothering her, trying her best not to look like a startled hare. "Why are we having this discussion in your suite?"

He sighed. "It's the only place Mama won't try to send some staff member to spy on us. And I need a shower before I can deal with the—"

"—mess I created," she automatically finished for him, wondering why Flora would involve herself in this when she usually stayed outside of Valentini company concerns.

"That was unfortunate phrasing on my part," he said, rubbing a hand over his temple. Was that regret that laced his words? That would have been strange enough to capture her focus, but something else stole and held her attention.

He leaned against the massive desk, stretching his long legs out in front of him. Custom-stitched Italian trousers pulled tight, displaying the hard lengths of his thighs. With that economy that imbued his every action, he undid the cuffs of his white dress shirt and slowly rolled each one back. The sight of his corded forearms, liberally sprinkled with hair, made Monica compulsively run her fingers over her own smooth forearms. Then his fingers went to his shirt and he unbuttoned a couple. Her pulse sped up, in direct proportion to each strip of olive-toned flesh that came into view.

His gaze snapped to hers and something else snapped into place between them. "It's not like you forced me to strip you in the middle of the piazza," he said, easily cutting through the growing tension. "Or made me carry you or begged to be transferred to a different department. I didn't handle that whole day well."

"Can I ask why?"

"Why what?"

"Why are you so…angry with me?"

"I'm not angry with you."

"You seem it. It's fair in a way, because I've brought your professional reputation into question. But it feels somehow…personal."

One hand thrusting through his hair, he stilled at her question. And while he only continued to stare at her thoughtfully, Monica realized his silence was assent.

It *was* personal. And then it came to her. "Is Mrs. Rossi upset by all this talk about our supposed affair?" How could she doubt a man like Andrea? "I'll talk to her and explain it all. Make it clear that there was never anything other than work between us. That all you've done is show me kindness, that you pitied me, that Flora forced you to—"

"Basta!" he said, looking even more disgruntled than before. "You're not some charity case. As to why I reacted badly, that's neither here nor there. Believe me, if Chiara was to be my fiancée, she would not doubt me."

"So she's not going to be your fiancée?"

"I have no interest in her, or in her father's deal when it comes with such strings. Especially when it's nothing but manipulation."

"You were never interested in marrying her?"

A soft, swift smile broke his serious expression, stealing Monica's breath. She flushed, reacting to that knowing glint in his eyes. Though she had no idea what the knowing was of. And then the other, bigger truth slammed into her.

"So all the hard work we put in for the merger is going to waste? All those jobs, that new manufacturing plant in Vienna…"

"Brunetti has always put his business before personal

life and family. It was the reason Papa never liked him. But that could be to our advantage right now. Chiara has always been a spoiled child and if she had told him that she and I were a sure thing, he would have attached her as an addendum clause, happy about the extra level of connection it would bring us. He would think nothing of abandoning her now, when he realizes I have no interest or intention of taking her on. Except it's become a…"

"A matter of pride that you have said no to his daughter. He wants the merger to go through but wants to save face as well," Monica finished his thought process.

"Exactly!"

She frowned. "I don't understand Mrs. Rossi's thinking. Why risk losing you by playing all these games? Why not be straightforward with you about her affections?"

He chuckled, though not quite to mock her. "You and Mama are peas in a pod."

Monica had no idea what he meant but she knew what she had to do. "I'll make a statement to the press immediately that the whole incident has been twisted and that I've been simply recovering at your mother's—"

"I thought you were terrified of talking to the press?"

"I am, but your reputation is not something I take lightly. I…"

"I have a different solution. One that would address *both* problems."

And here was the thing he'd clearly been reluctant to bring up, even as he'd made up his mind. Monica braced herself for anything, even though her heart ached at the thought of being sent away from Flora or Romeo or even…him.

Three weeks ago, as distressing as it had been, her transfer to a different department had felt necessary. To keep at bay all the feelings she'd discovered in her near delirious state.

But now, hearing this confirmation that Andrea had no interest in Mrs. Rossi, knowing that he cared about *her*, albeit in his own autocratic way, she didn't want to go away. She didn't want to stop working for him, or being near him. Which was really the pinnacle of the kind of foolish, clingy attachment she couldn't afford in a million years.

It wasn't as if anything could happen between them. So what was she doing feeling like this? Was she simply attaching herself to him because he was the most stable, genuine man she'd known in a long while? Why didn't she feel like this with Romeo, who was not only more handsome but also warm and open and approachable?

Something about him consumed her, as if finally, she had tuned in to the right frequency of her own heart and body. "What's the solution?"

"We will pretend that the story the tabloid press made up is true. That we've been in a relationship for months and that day, we had planned to elope to city hall but realized that Mama would be heartbroken at not being able to throw us a wedding. At the last minute, it became necessary to cancel it anyway because you were sick and had to be hospitalized. In two days, we'll arrive at a charity gala together. That will be enough of an announcement that we are together."

Try as she might, Monica couldn't muster up a response. Shock enveloped her so fully that all she could do was freeze and stare and…

Pretend they were together, that they'd been in a relationship for months. Go to a party with him. Pretend like she had the right to touch him, and kiss him, and want him...

Suddenly, she felt feverish all over again.

CHAPTER SIX

ANDREA'S HANDS CAME over her shoulders when she swayed. He smelled like pine and cloves and the deepest, darkest want she hadn't admitted to herself. His fingers on her flesh reminded her of the ache between her thighs when he'd touched her scar. Two more steps and her nipples would brush against his chest, and it was such an overload of sensory pleasure that she felt dizzy. The back of his hand came against her forehead. "Do you feel faint again?"

The pang of concern in his tone dissipated the shivers. God, she was acting like some Victorian virgin given to swoons at the slightest touch of a man. She needed distance, needed to fight the haze of desire he enveloped her in with his mere presence. Slowly, she edged back from his touch. "No, I'm fine. I just…"

"Ah…is the very idea of being affianced to me that frightening?"

"Of course not," she said, raising her gaze to him. "Are you sure you want to do this?"

"As sure as I can be."

"And it has to be an engagement? Not just…a fling." Just saying it made a lick of heat flash through her.

"If it's a fling, that just proves the media's point, no?

That I used you when you were under my power and then discarded you? An engagement also gives me armor against Chiara's mind games. Her father can come back to the table to discuss the merger without thinking that I rejected his daughter."

"Because you were already serious about me! And everything Flora said that day at the dinner to Mrs. Rossi adds up to it," she said, nodding. Then she blew out a breath that seemed to settle right between her throat and chest. "But what about Francesco?" Just saying his name made shame sit on her chest like a boulder. "He won't keep quiet when he hears this version. While he's not evil or anything, he'll try to twist this into some kind of gain for him and—"

"I will deal with him."

She raised a surprised gaze to him. "You will?"

"I'm Andrea Valentini. I have *some* resources available to me."

"As if anyone can forget who you are," she said, warmed by his attempt at humor.

Silence grew between them, gathering every twitch of her hands, every hitch of her breath, saying more than she wanted to say, betraying her.

"I know it puts you in an awkward position and I will understand if you refuse," he said, turning back toward his desk. When she didn't say anything, he gave a hard nod. "We will begin with the statement you can make to the press tomorrow and—"

"No, I...want to help sort this out. I want to pay you back in some small way for all the kindness you have shown me for four years."

He whirled around, every lean, hard inch of him radiating anger. "You will make a monster of me, just as the media says?"

"What? No. Why is it wrong to want to return—"

"Because if it was a kindness, then you insult Mama and Romeo and me by constantly talking about wanting to pay it back and—"

"No, that's now how I meant it. I had nothing and no one when I arrived here that summer on a whim. Now I have so much and I just want to contribute—"

"If that's why you want to do it, then let's stop now. If I had taken your overinflated sense of obligation into account, I'd have never considered it. Do you count us obligated to you since you nearly died to save Mama? What is the price for that?"

Frustration made Monica groan. Why was she botching this so badly, alienating him with her words? "I'm sorry for how I said it. I meant that if there's anything I can do to…help you out of this tricky situation, part of which I'm responsible for, I'm more than willing. I just can't help but wonder if you've thought this through."

"Three weeks with Romeo has shown you your claws, huh, *bella*?" His gray gaze swept over her face, as if he was seeing her anew. And yet, instead of irritation, admiration glinted there. "You never would have asked me that before."

"Yes, well. Humiliating life experiences have one upside to them. You're forced to think what's the worst that can happen and then come up with *Been there, went through that.*"

"This new boldness suits you," he said, and a thrill shot through her. "Now, tell me your reservations."

"I'm not…used to the high society you move in. Just

speaking to Mrs. Rossi—who was so sophisticated and poised—gave me the biggest fright. Luckily for us now, I couldn't mumble a word in my defense when she kept warning me to stay away from you. But I worry that I might cause your reputation more harm than good. I might be found out as an impostor of the worst kind. I know nothing of arts or fashion except for reading about them."

"All of those can be learned. You know enough about me, and that's more than most women, even Chiara, can say. Don't let anyone tell you you're less than who you want to be. Even me."

"Believe me, I'm trying," Monica said, liking this new, charming side of him as much as she liked the serious, ruthless side.

"*Bene.* What else?"

"This one's a big one." To avoid losing herself in those eyes, she started walking around the room, her pulse skyrocketing with every step she took. But she had to tell him. She had to make sure he understood before they got deep into this. "You might even decide that it's a deal breaker. But I…don't want to play games with you and I don't think I could, even if I tried. And I'm afraid it might just be—"

"Monica, what is it?"

His impatience made the words burst out of her. "I'm attracted to you!"

Dio mio, it was the last thing he'd expected her to own up to. And with such open, artless naiveté.

The primal attraction he'd felt toward her that day… It had taken him by shock, too. Still, he was experienced enough—Cristo, he'd thought his manly prowess was in winning as many women as he could as a cocky twenty-year-old race-car driver—to know that it wasn't one-sided. In the three weeks since he'd left her in his mother's care, he had wondered, multiple times, if she simply hadn't seen it. Or if she'd lied to herself that it didn't exist, since she also clearly believed that she was in love with that rogue. People clung to intrinsic beliefs like lifelines, even when the evidence to the opposite was in front of their eyes.

And here it was. The answer he'd desperately wanted to hear, delivered in such easy but complicated words.

Her arms were wound around her belly in a gesture of defensiveness that tugged at a part of him he hadn't known existed. *Dio mio*, did she think this attraction was wrong? As if everything around them and about them wasn't complicated already.

"Look at me, Monica."

It was the first time she defied his command, refusing to meet his gaze, continuing to walk around the study. "It feels…awful to feel all these things about you. And I don't even fully understand it. I've never felt like this before. Even with Francesco, it was never—"

"You don't need to draw a comparison chart, *bella*!"

She shook her head. "It could be that I'm just attaching to you because you were so good to me that day and I was half out of it. I had hoped these three weeks would be enough to wake me out of the trance but no, it's still there." She rubbed a hand over her neck and when his gaze went to the smooth column and the rising swell of her breasts, she pulled away from her own body, as if scalded. "It's still there and I am afraid that you…"

"Will take advantage of this...thing that you're not even sure about?" he bit out, his mind stuck on the word *awful*. She thought her attraction to him was awful? He hadn't required his masculinity or his ego to be validated on any basis in a long while, but *Dio mio*, if her assessment didn't rankle like a thorn stuck under his skin.

"What? No?" Alarm widened her big eyes. "I'm afraid that you might be...disgusted by me and my reactions and my little twitches every time you come near me when we put up this pretense of an affianced couple. I'm not sophisticated enough to play it all cool. Not that I would make a move on you. And I'm not even sure if this is some kind of reaction to Francesco and you're like this giant rebound blanket—"

"I would prefer it if you didn't bring that bastard up in our conversations."

She tilted her chin up, and then everything about her stilled. "You're angry with me again."

"It seems you're better at gauging my moods and my reactions than understanding your own feelings."

Now, when she should back off at his grumbly tone, she stayed put. "Why are you angry, Andrea?"

He sighed. "Let's just say my fragile ego got dented."

She smiled then, and it lit up her entire face. Those unique amber eyes of hers glowed with pleasure and he wondered how they would look full of desire. "That's not possible, is it? Will you not tell me? Please? If there's one constant, one anchor around me, it's you and where I stand with you. I'd like to—"

Andrea had to stifle his groan. If she used that pleading tone with him, he ran the risk of granting her whatever she wanted. "I'm not angry with you."

"More like frustrated?"

He shrugged. Then he asked the question he shouldn't. "Do you want to act on it?"

She looked as if he'd asked her to jump from a running train. Also something he'd attempted once to show off. She licked the curve of her thick, shapely lower lip, her pulse fluttering like a butterfly's wings at her neck. He wanted to press his mouth to that delicate spot, lick up the susurration and bite down on the sensitive skin, leaving a mark.

Usually, he preferred experienced partners, women who liked and demanded pleasure as much as he demanded his own. And here was this creature, looking like she might be blown off her feet by a strong kiss. So where was this coming from?

She was beautiful, yes, but simple beauty had never done it for him. Not since he'd finally grown up.

"What?" she whispered, her entire body trembling from head to foot now.

"Do you want to act on the attraction?"

"Why would you… What does that mean?"

"It means that this—" he motioned a hand between them, wondering at how convoluted this was "—is not one-sided."

"Oh! You mean you're attracted to me, too? You want…" Her mouth fell open on a soft gasp, her gaze finally, finally, landing on his mouth and staying there. "You want…"

"You. I want you."

She swallowed audibly.

He scoffed. "In case you haven't looked at a mirror recently, you're hot, *bella*."

"I'm a selection of symmetrical features and in-trend arbitrary body constructs that we've been programmed to like, but *you* are…" Her gaze moved over him—from his hair to his mouth to his neck to his chest—with a sweeping, overwhelming thoroughness, before she jerked it back up to his eyes.

"What? A slab of unfeeling rock?" he taunted, feeling as unbalanced and on edge as she seemed to be. Which made him wonder at how new this felt. "I would take you to my bed right now and give you what you want and demand you give me what I want, if you said yes. That's what I mean when I say acting on it. My only hesitation would be that I can't be a hundred percent sure Mama won't come banging on the door to protect her innocent lamb from me."

The reddish streak warming her cheekbones intensified as she pressed a hand to her mouth. "Flora knows."

"I think the entire goddamned world knows by now. Except you."

She walked toward him then, surprising him yet again. He could feel the pull between them as easily as if there were opposing poles embedded deep in their bodies. Her gaze, usually so meek, met his, pupils blown wide already. A breathless gasp left her as she seemed to find whatever confirmation she sought. Her hands fisted at her sides, and Andrea understood the need for that, too.

"This is a lot," she said, after what felt like an eternity stitched of hot, hungry moments.

"It is," he said, trying hard not to let his disappointment seep into his tone. "But chemistry is nothing but nature and instincts. It doesn't mean we have to give in to it."

"But you want to?"

He touched her then, just the pad of his thumb skimming over the soft, silky swath of skin on the inside of her wrist. Her pulse went haywire under his thumb, and her shallow breath was a symphony in his ears. "Yes. But it would be an affair, *a fling*, in your words. A…finite thing. I won't make false promises. I won't dress it up and call it dating. I won't lie and tell you that I'm interested in a girlfriend or a partner or a future wife. Because I'm not. I have no interest or any inclination toward love."

"How long would it last?"

He laughed then, and when she made a moue of her lovely mouth and made to pull away, he stopped her, all the while gentling his grip on her arm. She was so fragile in his hands. And more than just her wrist.

"Such anger, *bella*? I wonder that I know you at all, mouse."

Her catlike eyes flashed at him. "You're mocking me."

"I've…never been asked to fill out a questionnaire before I embarked on an affair."

Her eyes searched between his and then zoomed down to his mouth with a helpless eagerness that made him want to groan out loud. "And I've never just jumped into an affair with a man like…you."

"A man like me?"

"So out of my league. Who radiates confidence and sexuality and…"

Her open admission sent lust spiraling through him. *She was new to this and that meant it could go wrong in so many ways*, that rational voice he lived by whispered. "I wish I could put a shelf life on it. But I have no idea how long it would last. You might grow bored long before I do."

"Maybe in an alternate universe," she said, her own fingers coming to grasp the base of his palm in a tentative touch. He felt the contact shiver down his spine, wondering if he was so deprived of all touch or if it was just hers that had him reacting like this. Wondering if there would come a day when she realized the hold she could have over him.

"I guess the timing is convenient," she said, her voice gone husky.

"How?"

"The fake engagement, the forced proximity is a good cover to get it out of our systems." When he stared at her, she blushed. "That's the technical term."

He had never in his life discussed the terms of a maybe affair and the naiveté, the sheer lack of worldliness with which she asked the questions, told Andrea why his mother had been so outraged. Releasing her wrist, he moved away from her. "I tend to take people at face value. And yet, I cannot forget that you've just been through a painful, life-changing experience. And, by your own admission, you're not even sure what this is. What did you call me earlier? A giant blanket?"

"As much as I can cuddle a grumbly, grouchy bear," she said, coming up to the other side of the desk, her eyes wide in her face. When she gripped the edges of his desk and leaned over it, want made every inch of him curl tight.

He watched her, feeling a slow hum of pleasure through his veins at her aching beauty. Emotions flickered through her eyes. When the silence lengthened and he still didn't say anything, her mouth pinched down at the middle. "You're changing your mind about this. About wanting me."

He rubbed a hand over his face, feeling all of his thirty-four years in his bones. "No, I know I want you, Monica. And I know all the ways I want you. I cannot stop thinking of how many of my own rules I'm breaking by even admitting how much I want you."

"And if I said I was sure, Andrea? If I want to do this with you no matter what?"

"It *is* a lot. I should've never told you—"

"Then why did you?" she demanded, pushing her upper body over the desk like a bow bending toward him.

"Because I lost control. Your sweet admission made me forget how complicated all of this already is. When I invited you in here, all I meant to do was suggest the fake relationship. Not propose an affair."

"I know that. I started this. I was the one who said it first."

He stared at her, willing her to leave it, willing her to go.

"Do I need to sign a contract that says I won't ask for more than you give, or cling to you when it's done or that I'm old enough, wise enough and savvy enough to have sex with Andrea Valentini for pleasure without making it too much in my puny head?"

He let out a pithy curse.

She nodded, as if he had given her answers to all her questions. Then she wrapped her arms around herself again, as if she was pulling her dignity around her, and turned to leave. She was almost at the double doors when she turned back and said, "What time do we have to leave for the gala?"

"Monica—"

"We're not losing that contract. I'm not going to stop working for you because of something that didn't even happen, because of what that jackass did to me. And we're not going to let your reputation get tarnished." There was steel hidden in her quivering voice and it made him want her a little more.

She rubbed a palm over her flat belly and then glanced down at herself with a frown. "I need better clothes and shoes and maybe a little help with makeup."

"You're the most gorgeous woman I've ever met. And believe me, I have met some."

"Ri-i-i-ght," she said, stretching the word out. "I keep forgetting you had a playboy phase." Then as quickly as it came, the teasing left her eyes. "I don't want to let you down, Andrea."

"You won't."

"I don't want to let myself down, either. After everything with Francesco... I need a little boost of confidence. As the fake fiancée of the CEO of Valentini Luxury Goods, I'm allowed a little trip to the designer freebies showroom, aren't I? I've heard so many stories about it and I've been dying to go."

"Why didn't you just ask?" he said, then scoffed. "Right, the list of obligations and all that."

She nearly danced on the balls of her feet. "Can I, please?"

"Si."

"And just for the gala, can I have a stylist, and a makeup artist to help me get ready?"

"*Si*. Mama will arrange it for you."

"And who do I see for a little insight into how to seduce the man who's brilliant and ruthless and so gorgeous that he makes my knees quake even when he glares at me and calls me a damned headache?"

His mouth twitched and Andrea had to fight the insane urge to jump over the desk and tackle her to the floor. He would rip that ridiculous thing she called a top off her and bury his lips against her golden-brown flesh, dig his teeth into the curve of her breast, flick his mouth against the bold nipple that poked against the fabric even now, until she arched into him completely. Until she was begging for his mouth somewhere else.

The urge was overwhelming in its intensity.

Instead, he simply took in the breathtaking beauty of her, savored the thundering of his own pulse thrumming with a rich awareness he hadn't known in years.

He wanted to say yes to this, too. He wanted to say yes to anything she'd ask of him, if she asked him in that tone.

The little mouse was getting so bold. And it sent a thrill through him. Maybe he would never take her to bed, but *Cristo*, he felt like a new man when she flirted with him, when she crossed that edge of caution just for him, when she glared at him.

"You're growing bold."

She waved her fingers in the air, her eyes dancing with a wicked pleasure he'd never seen in her. Energy seemed to radiate from her, and he wondered if he was shortchanging her. If he was projecting the vague unease he felt at the back of his mind onto her. "Just flexing my newfound claws."

And then she was out the door.

For a long while Andrea stayed in his chair, wondering what he'd unleashed between them. And yet, there was not even a hint of regret to be found anywhere within him.

CHAPTER SEVEN

TWO EVENINGS LATER, Andrea stood waiting in the lounge of his family home, impatience and anticipation swirling through him in equal measure. He hadn't been this…invested in even the damned merger. But then, he knew the rules of that game. He'd written most of them.

With his assistant turned temptress…all bets were off. He felt as immature and unsure of himself as he'd felt with Chiara all those years ago. But for entirely different reasons.

For one thing, she was late.

Which was uncharacteristic enough of Monica that he couldn't help wondering if she'd changed her mind in the two days since they'd seen each other, since she'd declared with a steely resolve that she was going to be a part of the solution for the mess they had both had a hand in creating.

He wouldn't blame her if she did back out, though. He would even try to see it as the better outcome—notwithstanding the problem of Brunetti and the merger—because then he wouldn't have to spend God only knew how many months trying to avoid giving in to temptation.

How do I seduce a man who makes my knees quake?

Dio mio, that innocent and yet infinitely provocative question of hers had haunted him for two days and nights. An echo of her sunflowers-and-vanilla scent had lingered in the air long after she had left his bedroom. He'd woken up close to dawn, hard as nails, the sheets tangled around his lower body feeling like those fingers that had tingled against the base of his palm. *That* was all the contact they'd had and yet it felt like she had left the echoes of her tentative touch all over his body.

For the first time in years, he'd thrown off the sheets, sunk back into the bed and taken his erection in hand. Eyes closed, he'd spent long minutes running through the images of her in his head, like a slow reel he'd been saving up for his leisure.

The upswell of her breasts when she'd leaned over the desk, all anger and outrage that he was changing his mind. The lean, muscled lengths of her thighs as he'd carried her to the car. The relentless flutter of the pulse at her neck when he was close. The soft gasp that fell from her sensuous mouth when he touched her.

He flicked through every image while he pumped himself in his hand, reveling in the pinpricks of pleasure sparking all over his body and corralling down his spine, coalescing into a storm that made him thrust his hips up off the bed. The moment he reached the image of her gaze lingering on his mouth…he spilled all over his sheets, his climax a sudden, riotous explosion that had left him shaking.

For long seconds after, he'd lain against the sheets, his skin damp, his breaths bellowing through his lungs, lingering aftershocks making his muscles shake. It was a luxury of time, of experience, of mind and body, he never allowed himself anymore. Had not for more than a decade.

And as he'd gathered the sheets and thrown them into the laundry hamper, as he'd checked his phone like some gauche emo teenager after a first date to see if she'd texted him, as he'd padded naked into his shower and turned the water to an icy blast to cool down his overheated skin and suddenly rampaging libido, he wondered if that was why he was so attracted to Monica. Not just attracted, but attuned…in a way he had never been to another woman. If he'd deprived himself of even the smallest pleasures, like lying in bed thinking of a beautiful woman, of feeling the silk sheets against his skin, of the blood-tingling chase of wanting a woman, of letting his mind and body linger and revel in all that he'd built through sweat and tears.

He decided that was it, as a man who needed things to sit in clear, defined boxes. He'd been driving himself at a relentless speed, working eighty-hour weeks, pushing himself and the company and his staff to put out more products, more innovative designs, more investments, for thirteen long years…until Brunetti himself had reached out to him with interest in a merger. Driving himself toward another milestone, another million, another meteoric development, until his father's dream became true. Until he built enough wealth and power that Romeo and his mother would never need anything. Until Valentini Luxury Goods had become synonymous indeed with luxury and design and innovation. All the while, he… He had never learned to rest on his laurels, to celebrate his achievements, to simply enjoy the hardwon pleasures.

No wonder Brunetti's ridiculous condition had driven him to the brink so easily. No wonder he felt so…burned out. No wonder a delicate, inexperienced, almost fragile woman like Monica was catching him unawares, knocking him to his knees without even trying. God help him the day she decided she wanted to flex her sensuality, though.

"Andrea! What has come over you? That is the third glass of wine you have drunk in twenty minutes."

His mother's probing pulled Andrea out of the reverie. He turned to her and for the first time that evening noted the bright red lipstick, the complicated chignon, the navy blue designer dress and the simple diamond choker at her neck that had been a present from his father.

She was dressed up to the hilt, not something he'd seen in years. Her skin glowed with health and there was a simple joy to her gaze that made his heart swell in his chest. "What a beast I am, Mama, for not telling you how pretty you look this evening. Papa loved you in that color, I remember."

His mother blushed, scoffed and then slapped his arm, making sure he knew that she knew what he was doing. Romeo chuckled on her other side.

"*Grazie mile*, Andrea. But what is making you so restless that you drink so much?" At whatever she saw in his face, her words drifted away. "You are impatient to see her. You…like her. More than for—"

Andrea groaned. "Have we traveled in time back to my eighth grade, Mama?"

Turning so that she could see him fully, his mother clasped his cheek. He chafed under her scrutiny, not because he was thirty-four damned years old and she was trying to fix his hair, but because he couldn't bear to see the flash of grief the cut of his features usually brought her.

For all he teased Romeo about it, he was the one who looked so much like their father. He also remembered that, for almost a year after the accident, she'd been unable to look upon his face fully or meet his eyes or speak a sentence in his direction. Her grief at losing her husband had been so great that it had choked her to speak of their father for a long while. On some dark days, he'd even wondered if she hated him for causing the accident, if she would ever forgive him.

"Romeo reminded me that I am unfair to you," she said, her eyes shining with a suspicious sheen. "Judging you for this affair, real or fake, as if you were some… jungle predator, when in truth, you have not looked this interested in anything in a long time."

Andrea gritted his teeth, feeling more than discomfited under her scrutiny. "I would prefer it if you didn't discuss my personal stuff with him. Or with me. Or at all. There are certain things a man cannot continue to discuss with his mother."

"So it *is* personal?"

He groaned out loud.

She laughed and the soft sound snagged at his chest. "I forgot, momentarily, that you're your father's son, Andrea. That you would never knowingly hurt another. As for when it comes to your…manly affairs and desires… remember what he—"

"Mama," he groaned, clasping her cheeks in return. "This is worse than when Papa and you gave me the sex talk. At least then, I was remunerated for sitting through it."

His mother blushed but relented, nevertheless, by going on her toes to kiss his cheek. "I want you to be happy, Andrea. In whatever form it takes. I am sorry I... neglected you all these years."

"*Cristo*, Mama," Andrea said, enfolding her in his arms, his throat tight and aching. She was so small and had always been mostly unaware of the world's schemes, but hid a spine of steel. Just like another woman he knew. "I am a grown man and it is my turn to look after you. As it is Romeo's right, too."

She nodded, hiding her tears in his suit jacket. "I will not push you, but if you truly like her so much, why not turn this into a more—"

"You nicked yourself in two spots while shaving," Romeo said, coming to his rescue, his eyes full of devilish humor. "Mama's right. I haven't seen you drink a glass of wine that fast before, much less three, and now this. If it is this bad now, I cannot wait to see your condition once you two—"

Leaning away from his mother, Andrea pushed at Romeo's shoulder, hard enough that the wheelchair squeaked on the polished marble tiles. "*Basta!* You won't speak of her like that."

To the background of his mother's outraged gasp, Romeo not only recovered but also delivered a solid punch to Andrea's gut that he hadn't seen coming, and did so with a resounding cackle.

Eyes wide, his mother stared between them, and then shouted, *"Basta!"* just as Andrea decided to retaliate in kind. "You're behaving like dogs and I know your father and I have taught you better manners." At least she hadn't grabbed the tops of their ears and twisted them around like she used to do when they had been kids.

Whatever Andrea had been about to shout into Romeo's face died as a vision in pink appeared at the top of the steps of the circular balcony.

Her amber eyes widened, her pink mouth open on a gasp, Monica stared at Andrea's crooked jacket and Romeo's ruffled hair and Flora standing between them with her arms spread out like a referee at a particularly nasty soccer match. "What's going on?"

Andrea jerked his jacket down, his head feeling woozy as if he'd received a pounding to his head rather than to his gut. In a hot pink sleeveless dress that hugged her breasts and then flared out from under them, Monica looked like some lush, exotic flower at full bloom. The rich pink made her shoulders and neck gleam like burnished gold, while the upper swells of her breasts rose and fell with her shallow breaths. With each step she took down the stairs, the almost thigh-high slit bared the lean length of her thigh, her legs even longer than usual in gold-strapped stilettos that Andrea had to swallow and look away from, counting his breaths. Her dark, silky hair had been curled into long waves and they slithered over and away from her chest, as if beckoning him for a closer look.

She neared them and a subtle scent overlaid with her own hit his nostrils.

"What's happening?" she asked, slowly but definitely moving toward Romeo.

Andrea gritted his teeth, while his brother wriggled his brows in a childish taunt, meant for him.

Monica's hands went to Romeo's ruffled hair and in a smooth move, she pushed at the thick, wavy strands until they settled back into his designer haircut. Jealousy at the open affection clung to Andrea's throat like the thick brew Mama used to make them drink to ward off colds.

"The Valentini brothers forgot that they're full-grown men and instead decided to fight like ruffians." His mother took the younger woman's hand and pulled her close for a better look. "You look beautiful, *cara*. I know you're nervous about this whole…drama that you and Andrea are cooking up, but do not be, *si*? Anyone who talks to me and Romeo will know that we wish it were the truth."

Alarm flickered through her eyes but Monica nodded. Still not meeting his eyes. "Thank you. I want to be of help."

"You've always been more than that to me," his mother said, tapping Monica's cheek. Then she stepped back and gave her a once-over. "I would recommend a piece of jewelry with your outfit but I will leave that in Andrea's capable hands."

As he watched, Romeo pulled Monica to him and kissed her on the cheek—a little too close to the corner of her mouth for Andrea's liking, but he had already given his far too intrusive family too much ammunition against him. Then his brother whispered something in her ear that made her cheeks flush the same color as her dress.

A slow, thunderous beat seemed to take up in his blood as his mother and Romeo left the lounge, intending to arrive at the gala separately from him and Monica. Finally, when Monica set that liquid gaze on him, something he couldn't recognize shimmered there. Her slender arms spread in a welcoming stance, she asked, "What do you think? Will I do as Andrea Valentini's fiancée?"

"What did Romeo say to you?" he bit out, instead of acknowledging her question.

Her expression shuttered and her chin rose with that willful streak he was coming to recognize and like. Although not so much at this particular minute. "That's between me and your brother."

Cristo, no wonder his family was teasing him like they did. He behaved like a hormone-ridden, angsty teenager around her. And he should have known she'd clam up when he demanded an answer to such an inane question.

In nearly two years of working intimately for him and with him, she had never cowered or bent at his criticisms or his demands or his perfectionist, workaholic tendencies. She didn't engage in an argument, but always brought him around to her point of view in the end. Slowly, but surely, as she was driving him out of his mind now.

Sighing, he said, "Mama is right. We need jewelry for you."

He didn't wait to see if she followed him, leading the way to his father's old study. Like his mother had rightly guessed, he'd already had a jewelry showroom that he knew Chiara had always liked send him some pieces in advance. Now he regretted not asking Romeo to look through the selection and eliminate the worst options. He knew nothing of the current trends in jewelry—design and fashion had always been Romeo's field of expertise—nor of Monica's tastes. But there were at least a dozen pieces for her to pick from.

He turned to find her looking around with wide eyes.

The study was a remnant from his father's time and while Mama constantly asked him to redo it, he hadn't found the heart to erase memories of his father.

"This is different from your study at work. Or upstairs," she said, not meeting his eyes. "It's so full of… character and charm."

Beyond the smooth, silky skin of her shoulders, he saw the tightness with which she held herself. And Andrea suspected he had hurt her by not complimenting her, even after she'd specifically asked it of him. A part of him found it maddening that he couldn't give her a simple compliment that she could appreciate, but a bigger part of him was almost resentful of her for reducing him to such peevish behavior.

"It was Papa's," he said, gentling his tone. "He was an avid reader and a fan of woodworking. Many of the pieces are his."

She nodded, her long neck tilting forward to look at the pieces up close. "He was very talented."

"*Si.*"

"But this one…" She bent and leaned close and Andrea didn't look away fast enough to miss the delectable sight of how the silk moved over the swell of her buttocks.

She touched the one he had carved of a wood nymph from a dark wood that Romeo had acquired from some trader a couple of years after Papa's death. In turn, Andrea had put a sketchbook into his brother's hands, determined to provoke him from the deep, dangerous fugue state Romeo had slipped into. It was the first step they had both taken to carve their way back to each other and to life itself.

While Andrea had worked on that particular piece during the nights Romeo had sketched, he hadn't taken it up again since. Not until this past year. He had had very little time for woodwork, after he'd taken over the company full-time, especially when all his risks and strategies had exploded it beyond even his own vision.

Or was that another lie he had told himself?

Maybe because it was the one thing where he and his father had seen eye to eye, had understood each other, had met each other without the usual frustration and animosity that had colored their relationship when he'd turned eighteen and his ambitions and vision for life had veered completely away from his father's dreams for him.

"This is yours," she said, awe in her tone.

"How do you know that?" he said, his voice sharp from the sudden, overwhelming flush of pleasure that bathed him. When she didn't answer, he said, "Answer me."

She turned, but her arms crisscrossed over her belly in a defensive posture he hated. "The style is different from the others. Also similar to the almost finished one, the mermaid that you keep hidden away in your drawer at work. The detail in such a tiny piece is…magnificent."

"You went snooping?"

She stood ramrod, her eyes going wide. "Of course not. I was just curious if you had—" now she was blushing again "—liked it."

"What do you mean?"

Her lush mouth puffed out in a frustrated exhale. "I was snooping, *si*. Fire me for my sins."

"I have worse punishments in mind if you don't give me the answers I want, Ms. D'Souza."

A lick of heat dawned through her yellow eyes, making them burn bright and hot. An answering heat punched through Andrea, knowing that she understood him, knowing that her mind had gone there just as his did.

"That would have frightened me a few months ago, Mr. Valentini. Now whatever you deal out..." She swallowed, the pulse at her neck thrashing at her own boldness. "I'm more than willing and ready."

He cursed. "Tell me, *per piacere*."

Even his "please" was apparently not enough. Her gaze searched his, looking for reassurance, he thought. Finally, she sighed and gave in. "I asked Romeo what you might appreciate for your birthday last year and he told me about your hobby. That dark African wood..." Her words came out rushed now. "I found a dealer online and had it shipped. But it was so expensive that I could only afford a small piece. For weeks after, I was curious to see if you'd worked on it. Even then, I didn't snoop on purpose. I... You gave me the locker combination one night eight months ago in the middle of the Japanese buyout and it was there. Not fully formed and yet already incredibly beautiful in the promise emerging. I couldn't help going back to check on its progress."

"Why?" he asked, floored by her admission. He had assumed the gift had been Romeo's doing.

"Why what?"

"Why did you ask Romeo?"

"Am I not allowed to gift you a small thing, Andrea?" Her tone was soft, whisper-thin, but the thrust of her question so deep and precise that he found himself floundering.

"Why didn't you just contribute to the staff pool?" he said, sounding churlish to his own ears.

"I… I wanted to give you something meaningful. Do you remember how Flora had been sick for weeks with that cough and we worried it might be pneumonia?"

"*Si.* You stayed with her and nursed her through four nights. Through the worst. Romeo said you slept in that armchair."

She shook her head. "That was nothing. You… You were so worried about her and I wanted to—" she licked her lips again "—make you feel better, I guess. Obviously, I couldn't afford any of the good stuff like your favorite liquor or cuff links or a tie. But when Romeo told me you used to woodwork quite a bit… I was surprised and went researching."

"*Grazie* for the gift," he said, staring at her in spiraling consternation. "It distracted me from…everything."

Resentful bastard that he was, he didn't tell her that it had done so much more. It had brought him back to his hobby again. To the thing he had shared with his father and loved. Even to a part of himself that he had lost. He had worked on two more pieces since then and even commissioned a woodworking shed to be built on his property. Something that had remained only a dream for his father.

Her throat moved on a swallow as she nodded. "I'm glad. When I saw the finished piece, I realized Romeo hadn't been exaggerating out of brotherly love."

He laughed at that, as she intended him to. And he wondered how much she must have managed his moods, his uneven temper in the throes of a project or his demands and his criticism, without his noticing it for so many months. "As you probably know by now, he is the very opposite. More along the lines of my critic and my mirror," he said, meeting her eyes again.

Her teeth dug into her lower lip, her eyes flaring with understanding. "I appreciate that he looks out for me. But he also knows I need to make my own decisions, right or wrong. Even the stupid ones."

Luckily for them both, his watch beeped before he could pick up the gauntlet she threw down and pounce on her right there in what had been his father's study. "We will be late. Take a look and pick what you want," he said gruffly.

Dutifully, she sauntered toward the dark mahogany desk where everything from necklaces to diamond studs were lying open in dark green velvet cases. She gasped. "I… These are real diamonds and sapphires and…emeralds. I can't pick one out of these. If you really think I need jewelry, I have some costume jewelry pieces in my—"

"That won't do for my fiancée," he said, taking her wrist in his hand and tugging her forward when she staggered back. "And you promised to accept a gift or two from Mama, remember?"

"Yes. But these aren't from your mother. These are from you. And way too expensive."

He sighed. "Do not turn this into a fight."

"Do not order me around, then."

When he turned to face her, she gripped the desk and stayed where she was. Her beauty hit him with the force of a tsunami. "This will never work if you won't accept gifts from me. Or if you jump every time I touch you."

"I didn't jump. I just… I've never been so aware of another person's…nearness. I'm trying, Andrea."

As if to prove her point, she covered the distance between them until a flying lock of her hair hit his chest. This close, he could see the yellow-amber flecks in her big eyes. Could see the tiny beads of moisture over her upper lip.

"Let's make a deal. If you grant me what I ask for," she said sweetly, "I'll pick a piece and be the most obedient fiancée you could ever want."

Every muscle turned flint-hard in his body. "What do you want, *bella*?"

"One of your sculptures."

"What?" he repeated, as if he was hard of hearing.

"If you promise me one of your sculptures, then I'll accept one piece of jewelry tonight. I won't even try to return it."

"That's the most ridiculous negotiation I've ever witnessed."

"I don't care what you think," she said, setting her mouth into that mulish set. "I want what I want."

"Give me one good reason why."

"Those are beautiful and they're a piece of you. A piece of Andrea Valentini that only a few know. A piece I will cherish for a long time, whatever and wherever this farce leaves us."

With that simple request, she reminded Andrea exactly who she was and who she would always be. Of how a fundamental part of her makeup meant she'd always see the world in terms of emotions he could not afford. She was already asking for pieces of him that he was loath to part with and soon, she'd ask for something he couldn't give.

Cristo, she was far too innocent and good for the likes of him. She had no idea what an affair with him would cost her. And as much as he hated to admit it, he was… *fond* of her in a way that precluded ruining his relationship with her by adding sex to it.

Suddenly, he hated the very idea of having to parade her in front of guests and friends and family, letting them stare her up and down as if she was a prime cut of meat. He hated the idea of anyone destroying that fragile, deep-rooted sense of kindness and generosity with which she greeted the world.

"Bene," he said, turning her around to face the necklaces with a hand on her shoulder. "It is a done deal. You'll have one sculpture of my choice. Now, choose something."

Leaning forward, she bumped her side into his front, pointing to the farthest one in the top corner. He should have guessed that it would be her choice, given it was the most delicate and smallest of the lot. He almost pointed out to her that it was the most expensive one, given its intricate flower and leaf-like work with platinum and tiny high-carat diamonds by one of the most exclusive jewelry designers in all of Italy. He'd only been able to acquire it because the designer was a friend of Romeo's.

"Turn around," he ordered briskly, once he had the delicate thing in hand.

When she tugged her hair away from the nape of her neck, he noticed the expanse of smooth, silky flesh exposed by the plunging cut of the dress in the back. Instant goose bumps rose on her flesh and the most overwhelming impulse to run his mouth down the line of her spine rode him hard.

Hands shaking, as if he had been whittling away at wood for hours, he clipped the necklace at her nape. Then without meeting her eyes, he checked his watch and barked out that they were late, thanks to her arguments.

Determined not to feel her hurt as she tried to keep up behind him, he turned himself into one of those sculptures he carved. He wanted her too much to keep this in his control and she... *Madre mio*, she was made for a different kind of man.

CHAPTER EIGHT

It HAD BECOME astoundingly clear to Monica over the ever-stretching evening that she was a complete disaster on her first outing as Andrea Valentini's fiancée.

Beginning with the moment they had entered the huge ballroom, when she had immediately drawn the eyes of every guest. Which was bad enough, because, in her determination to help Andrea out of this mess, she'd forgotten how much she disliked being the center of attention. And being Andrea Valentini's fiancée meant all the eyes of the Milanese high society would be on her.

When she'd frozen at the top of the steps to the huge ballroom, Andrea had gently rubbed her hip with his fingers, his expression patiently inquiring. It was the patience, as if he were afraid that she might fall apart, that had her straightening her spine. Especially when she knew he was not happy with her.

He hadn't liked it that she knew about his hobby earlier or that she'd demanded a piece of his art. She'd known that he was an intensely private man but she hadn't thought she'd come up against a boundary that soon. He'd been quiet all through the drive to the gala, barely even meeting her eyes. So the downfall of the evening had begun even before they had arrived.

Then, with each step they took, she sensed something off in the large room with its high domed ceiling and crystal chandeliers. Once people began to flock toward them and Andrea began introducing her, she got it. Everyone was dressed in very somber navy blues and beiges and even browns. The only splash of color she'd seen other than her own was a dark purple belt on one of the navy blue dresses.

Why hadn't he asked her to change when she'd shown up in the garish pink thing from the freebie closet at the Valentini design studio? Why hadn't he told her that the charity gala was a sober affair?

She looked like a weed—wild, overgrown, forced to bloom an unnatural color by fertilizer—among the rows and rows of perfectly manicured prize flowers. That had thrown her off completely. Even then, she might not have cared, could have simply told herself that no one would expect poise or sophistication of the gauche, awkward American Andrea had saddled himself with. Only, after the awkward dance where she hadn't been able to shed the embarrassment and had more than once trampled on his feet and slammed into him with her full body, Andrea had begun progressively freezing her out. To which she had reacted by spilling champagne over herself. After that, she'd barely held off tears.

The worst part, Monica told herself, rubbing at the already spreading stain of champagne from near her boob, was that Andrea had spent the rest of the evening with his ex. She'd have preferred if somehow Mrs. Rossi had been responsible for Monica's various faux pas through the evening. But all the woman had done, having been seated at the same table as her and Andrea, had been to answer his questions about a mutual friend's wedding. Their conversation had progressed from there naturally. Clearly, Mrs. Rossi had learned from her mistake and was trying to correct it, even at this stage.

Not that anyone would blink an eyelash if Andrea announced tomorrow morning that a connection had been reignited with his ex and he was dumping the little mouse. So here she was, emerging from the restroom, where she had tried her best to get rid of the stain and only ended up smearing it across the fabric, to find Andrea dancing with Mrs. Rossi.

Monica stilled, the flash of Andrea's genuine smile piercing her skin like a thorn even across the ballroom. Whatever embarrassment she had felt through the evening weighed nothing in comparison to the hurt she felt at seeing him happy with his ex.

She wondered if whatever attraction he'd admitted to feeling for her had already passed under the weight of something older, deeper and more real. And she knew that she had to get away before she made an even bigger fool of herself.

Andrea barely waited for the lift car to open as he stepped into his penthouse. He'd never been so angry with Romeo before, not even when they had constantly fought in their younger years—so badly that Papa had to threaten them with dire punishments.

To calmly and quietly send Monica away from the gala, without even telling Andrea…it was a miracle he hadn't lost his temper. All he'd wanted was to run after her, but somehow, he'd kept his common sense. The annual charity gala was to honor his father, to raise funds to donate to a children's charity that had been close to Papa's heart.

It would have been the height of distaste for Andrea to leave the guests. So he had bidden his time. For a while, a very short while, he'd even forgotten about her absence thanks to an interesting conversation with Chiara, who had made a smart turnaround and admitted that she'd considered him an easy prize and persuaded her father to add her as a clause.

It had been both refreshing and unsurprising to know that after all these years Chiara hadn't lost her ambition or her ability to see through to his mood. Just when he'd spent almost five minutes without thinking of his fleeing assistant, she'd dipped her head toward him and whispered, "I don't remember seeing you this out of sorts even when I announced my engagement."

He had nothing to say to that because *he was*, over a slip of a woman who kept surprising him at every turn.

He scanned the expansive lounge that gave a three-sixty-degree view of the living room, dining space and the kitchenette, and beyond it the glittering lights of Milan, to find it empty. Monica's pink dress was lying on the plush leather sofa under the glare of a tall designer lamp. Then he saw her, his assistant slash fake fiancée, on the floor, on her knees, her white teeth gritted tight.

Her long, wavy hair hung in a thick, loose braid down her back. Andrea had the most insane fantasy of wrapping that thick braid around his hand while he... As if aware of his filthy thoughts, she turned around.

"What the hell are you doing on the floor?" he asked, barely restraining his temper.

"Andrea…what are you doing here?" Her eyes were wide in her face and a little red-rimmed.

The passing thought that she might have been crying only made his answer sharper. "Seeing as this is *my penthouse*, my private space, that is my question, *si*?"

"Fair enough," she said, and shied her gaze away. When she tugged a thread and bit it off, he realized she'd been sewing the hem. Then, with infinite care, she folded the dress into a garment bag and pushed to her feet.

He stared.

She was wearing a white dress shirt, *his shirt*, the cuffs folded to her elbows but still falling down to cover her fingers. Since she was almost as tall as he was, the edges fell to her thighs and *Dios mio*, her legs went on and on. With a few buttons undone, he could see the silky swath of her neck and chest and all he wanted was to touch and kiss and lick her.

Picking up the bag, she walked toward him. "I never meant to invade your privacy. I thought Romeo was sending me to his friend's place. If you can call a cab, I'll get out of your way."

"Not before you tell me why it was so important that you leave the gala. Are you already regretting making all those promises to me?"

He sounded so irate that he could see her mouth tremble, then stiffen to a taut line. "I wanted to leave before I embarrassed you even more."

It was the last thing he'd expected her to say. And he could see the truth of it in her face. Why was it that suddenly they were on two different wavelengths? Why the hell was this so…hard? "I never said that you embarrassed me."

"It was only a matter of time. Two minutes in, I knew it was the most ridiculous plan. We should have never..." She swallowed and met his gaze. "Will you call a cab for me, please?"

"And where will you go dressed in my shirt, looking like you do, *bella*? Crying into Romeo's arms again? You reach for him even as you tell me you can take me on."

Frustration and something more danced across her face. "Fine, he's become a safety net. I'll sleep on the sofa here and before you're up, I'll be gone. Then—"

"Why are you upset, Monica? Why leave without telling me?"

"I told you, I didn't—"

"And I have told you that I wasn't embarrassed by you and—"

"How the hell would I know that?"

"You know me well enough to know I would tell you if you were embarrassing me, *bella*."

"Would you? Andrea, I trod on your feet during the dance and I slammed into you twice so hard it's a miracle I didn't take us both to the floor for everyone to laugh at. And then I dropped a glass of champagne on myself during the silent bidding and there was the fact that I looked like a tacky weed among your guests and my God, why didn't you tell me the gala was to honor your father and—"

He pressed his hand to her mouth and felt her warm exhale. "Tacky weed? What has that got to do with the fact that it was to honor my father and—"

She shoved his hand aside but he refused to let her go. "I dressed like I was the main act at a carnival. Didn't you see how I stood out among the others? I never thought you a liar, of all things."

"I did notice how you stood out, *si*," he said, taking the garment bag from her and throwing it aside. "How does that make me a liar?"

"Because you're pretending now as if nothing was wrong," she said, pink cresting her cheeks. "You could barely look at me the entire time we were dancing and then the rest of the dinner, you were deep in conversation with your... Mrs. Rossi. You know, it's not too late."

"Not too late for what?"

"You could claim that this was all a misunderstanding and you realized that you and she have...reconnected. It was clear that you are..."

"We are what?"

"You will make me say it? Make me sound even more foolish?"

"*Si*. I do," he said, unrelenting.

"You enjoyed her company so much that you ignored 'your fiancée.' You could barely look at me after you two struck up a conversation. What was I going to do? Sit there with a stained dress and let everyone see how miserable and jealous I felt?"

Admission of jealousy would have sent him running if it had been anyone else. But with her... Andrea wanted to understand it. "So instead of confronting me about it, or demanding that I pay attention, you hid behind Romeo? Did you think for a second how it would look that my fiancée ran away from me?"

"Demand your attention?" she said, eyes wide, as if it was such an alien concept that most of Andrea's anger melted away.

"Is that so shocking?"

"When you would barely look at me, yes."

Andrea cursed. "I know I'm closed off enough to make a lover feel ignored. And I take full responsibility for our crossed signals tonight. But you know me, Monica. You know I'm not so fickle as to change my mind about you or to lose myself in Chiara all of a sudden. So explain to me why it is so hard for you to demand attention when it is your right."

"You want to know? Really?"

Some hard shell that had formed around his heart broke open at her shocked tone. Did she expect so little from him, for herself? He ran a hand over her cheek, feeling that intense protective urge again. "Yes, *bella*."

"I'm not used to…attention," she said, her mouth pinched. "All my life, I've done my best to deflect it, to keep away wandering eyes and hands. When we walked into the ballroom, all those eyes on me…it was like my worst nightmare come true. I desperately didn't want to disappoint you and then I went and did exactly that because I was so anxious with all the attention."

"Why didn't you tell me that?"

"It took me four years and a near-lethal rash and a botched wedding to admit that I… I'm attracted to you. But before we left your house, you…didn't like that I encroached on your personal life."

Andrea rubbed a hand over his jaw, knowing she was right. Guilt settled like a hard weight on his chest. "I'm not used to sharing personal stuff."

"I know that. But you barely even paid me a compliment, although I know now it's because I dressed like—"

"I didn't compliment you because you rendered me

speechless. I avoided looking at you because I wanted nothing more than to take you to the floor, as you put it, and have my wicked way with you, right there for the entire world to see. As for standing out, you would have stood out if you had gone there wearing what you are in now, *bella*. There was not a person there that doubted why the ruthless mogul, Andrea Valentini, was suddenly, secretly engaged to a woman out of nowhere. No one who saw you this evening could doubt how much I want you."

"Oh…" she said, pink tingeing her cheeks. "You really liked me in that dress? It wasn't too much?"

"However you dress, whatever you say, you are never too much, *bella*."

"This event, going out as your…fiancée…felt like a safe way to put myself out there, to try something new. But it was hard. And then when I learned that the gala is to support a foundation that was very dear to your father… I wondered why even Flora didn't tell me to change."

"Because, like me, Mama found nothing wrong with how you dressed. Chiara might have turned her snotty nose up at you but that's because she knows she can't carry that color."

A frown marred her brow and Andrea knew there was more. A thread of tenderness wrapped tight around his chest at how little she expected of the world while still meeting it with all the generosity she could muster. "Mrs. Rossi… You genuinely seemed to enjoy her company. I won't stand in the way of something real and good and—"

"My overwhelming reaction when you walked in this evening looking like you do and my jealousy about how close you are to Romeo… It made me angry with myself." He thrust a hand through his hair, knowing she deserved more. Vulnerability, he could not do, but honesty, he could. "I'm not used to being out of control and I don't share what's in my head easily."

"But you and—"

He clasped her cheek then, forcing her to look at him, hating that he had caused her so many doubts. "Chiara knew me well enough to see I was having a tantrum and teased me about it."

"Teased you? About what?"

"That, uncharacteristically, I was denying myself something I really wanted, that I suddenly possessed an overdeveloped sense of honor."

Her yellow eyes met his, her breath a sudden rasp in the quiet. "Honor… Ah, yes. Because you pity me. You think I'm not strong enough to handle you. Or she's wrong and you just don't want this at all." She stood close enough that he could smell the faint scent of vanilla and sweat, could see the drops of perspiration on that bow-shaped upper lip. "All I asked Romeo was to—"

Andrea tugged her to him suddenly enough that her chest slammed into his. His own breath punched out of him at the delicious press of her soft curves. "You should have told me you wanted to leave. Not him."

Her gaze searched his, some new understanding dawning there. "You don't like it when I ask you for things."

It was close enough to the uncomfortable truth and yet he couldn't back down. "That's not—"

"Maybe because you think I'll ask for too much or because—" she tilted her chin up, her openly wanting gaze hitting him square in the gut "—you're afraid you can't truly give me what I need. Maybe this is not about me at all."

"The little mouse is turning into a cat with claws?"

She shrugged and the shirt fell off, revealing one smooth brown shoulder. "Or I'm realizing that I should stop pursuing men who think I'm not good enough for—"

"I will give you what you want, *bella*," he whispered, his words thick with desire. "Anything you want. Ask me, Monica."

She didn't say anything for so long that Andrea thought she'd lost her nerve. Then she exhaled and her hands came up to clasp his cheeks and she brought that luscious mouth to his. That first soft press of her lips against his drained away all the anger he'd felt at her leaving and all the resolve he'd shored up the entire evening to resist her.

Yes, this would only be a fling, but she knew the score and who the hell was he to decide what she could or could not handle?

He had behaved like a donkey's ass all evening— ignoring her, cursing himself for the possessiveness he felt—but the moment he had realized she had left, he'd known it was useless to try to resist this heat between them. He wanted her too much.

Her kiss was gentle and exploratory, as if she still didn't believe that he wouldn't push her away. When Andrea pulled his head back, she followed with a protest, lips clinging to his, fingers digging deep into his shoulders to keep him tethered to her. A chuckle emerged from his chest but she swallowed that, her mouth opening wider, her tongue swiping at his with tentative but wanton strokes. Her fingers went to the nape of his neck, the tips digging into his hair and pulling, and when she pressed herself flush against his body and moaned, every little lie he'd told himself collapsed.

Wrapping his arm around her waist, Andrea tugged her to him. A soft *oof* escaped her mouth as he circled her nape and tilted her mouth just so for his liking. *Dio mio*, she was sweet like the thickest of honeys and responded like quicksilver. When was the last time he'd known such pure, sweet passion, the last time he had even allowed a woman to touch him with such abandon, the last time he'd truly looked for a connection and not just easy sex?

"More, please, Andrea. More," she whispered against his lips.

He ravished her mouth, desire licking through him like an inferno, as she responded to every stroke and lick and nip without backing down, demanding in that breathy little voice that he not stop. When he sucked on the tip of her tongue, her nails dug into his nape, egging him on. He didn't remember the last time a kiss had revved him up this fast; didn't remember when it had become the end rather than the means.

He could have gone on kissing her for the rest of the night, if that was all they could have. He felt dizzy like he used to when he'd beaten a previous speed or taken to a new racetrack and broken records.

Slowly, he pulled back, their breaths choppy and fast around them. Pupils blown wide enough to eat up the unique yellow, Monica clung to him.

Andrea kept his hand around her neck, loving the way she burrowed into his touch, loving how she molded herself against him like a climbing vine, loving how she trembled from head to toe. Finally, she looked up, and a lazy smile stretched her swollen lips. Without looking at him, she rubbed the pad of her thumb against his lower lip, the touch exploring and gentle.

Andrea opened his mouth and sucked the digit in. Her rough rasp sent his blood pooling south. He released her finger with a pop.

"That was…" She blinked, pulled back and searched his gaze. "That was the best kiss I've ever had," she said, chin risen almost belligerently.

"If you're looking for disagreement," he said, his hands stroking over the planes of her back, loving how she pushed toward him, seeking more, "you will not find it here. Tell me, *bella*, did you get what you wanted?"

She nodded. Then, leaning forward, she pressed her cheek against his and rubbed, like a cat. Her skin was like the softest velvet against his rough jaw, and slowly, as if in beat to his drugged pulse, she brought her mouth to his ear and said, "Yes, but I'm greedy, Andrea. I want more."

"Spell it out for me."

"I want to go to bed with you. I want to touch you as I've wanted to for three weeks. I want to see if reality can stand up to my feverish, delirious dreams of you. I want to explore this between you and me and I want so much pleasure that I—"

His hands on her hips, Andrea picked her up and she instantly wrapped her arms around his back. He kissed her roughly, deeply, even as he maneuvered through the lounge to his bedroom. He bit her lip and when she jerked against him, nudging her sweet core against his thick shaft, he told her in filthy words all the stuff he'd wanted to do to her the moment he'd seen her in the dress earlier that evening; all the things he'd thought when she'd slammed into him during the dance; all the possessiveness that had swirled through him when she'd danced with a colleague who had a reputation for wandering hands.

CHAPTER NINE

MONICA WOULD HAVE floated on the fluffy clouds of sensation from his kiss for the rest of the night, if not for Andrea gently lowering her to what felt like another cloud. It was his bed, she realized, her heart fluttering in her chest like a hummingbird's wings. Then there was a sudden explosion of light and she scrunched her eyes shut, fighting it and the urge to hide herself.

"Monica?"

From his soft tone, she knew that he'd seen her momentary hesitation. His hands rubbed over her arms, gentling her. "It can just be a kiss."

God, what a coward she was.

She opened her eyes to find him looking down at her. Her breath hung suspended in her chest at the sight of him like this, with her, for her. Out of the periphery of her vision, she took in the vast bedroom with all-glass walls on two sides, giving a delicious peek out into the night glitter of Milan. And inside, she was aware of the sheer luxury of the silk sheets under her hands, the vaulted ceilings and the airiness of the space. But all of it was a background hum to the main attraction, the man whose attention she held now.

This was not the Andrea Valentini that the world got

to see, with his hair all mussed, and his thin, sculpted mouth just a little puffed up from her kisses, and his dark, dark eyes betraying his desire. This was the Andrea she'd conjured in her dreams and for a second, Monica felt a frantic pulse of panic thrash through her that she couldn't handle him in reality, that she might not be enough to hold his attention for more than… Which made her even more desperate to grab this moment and enjoy it to the fullest. She shooed away all those niggles and, leaning back onto her elbows, drank him in, letting her senses fill her up with him.

He was a feast to her eyes with scruff on his cheeks, his shirt unbuttoned enough for her to see the shadow of taut olive-colored skin stretched tight over his chest. Unlike Francesco, who had been very proud of his gym body and his waxed chest and oiled muscles, Andrea was lean and taut. There was an effortlessness to his masculinity, a raw, innate confidence that established him as a natural leader.

"Any more doubts, *bella*?" he asked, a twinkle in his eyes. But he wasn't laughing at her; she knew that, too.

"Nope. Nada. Zilch," Monica replied, sitting back up. Reaching him, she unbuttoned his shirt all the way and pushed it back onto his shoulders. His chest was covered in a smattering of hair. Fingers trembling, she traced the contours of his torso, from the corded column of his throat to the hard pectorals, all the while loving the graze of his hair against her palm. Just touching him made desire beat louder in her veins, and she never wanted to stop. Never had she felt this kind of desire to make a man crave her as much as she did him.

When she reached his leather belt, she hesitated, but

slowly pushed on, undoing it first. His fingers arrested her. Bringing her hand to his mouth, Andrea pressed a kiss to her wrist. "My turn." And then he tugged the lapels of her shirt up in his hands and tore them apart until the few buttons she had managed flew off and pinged on the cold marble floor.

"Will you let me do what I want with you, *bella*?"

"You don't have to test me anymore," she said, watching him with greed.

He grinned then and bent over her, licking the shell of her ear. "When I found that you'd left the party without telling me, I was so angry with you. All I could think of on the ride over here was how I would torment you for leaving."

Startled by the possessive edge of his words, Monica looked up. The intensity of his gaze only made her skin feel tighter. She rubbed her thighs together but didn't find even a bit of relief. "You're not going to scare me off. Do to me what you will. Just…tell me what I can do, too, please. I want to please you, Andrea."

If he heard the doubts in her voice, he didn't mock her for them. Bending, he pushed the shirt off her shoulders and took her mouth with a rough need she understood very well. Then he took her hand and brought it to his crotch.

A needy gasp escaped her mouth as she felt the hard length of his shaft against her palm. She instantly cupped him, driven by an instinct that told her everything about this encounter was going to turn her inside out, change her, ravish her.

But God, she was so ready for it, for him. "You are already blowing my mind, *bella*. I've been walking around with an erection most of the evening, like some uncontrollable adolescent."

"I'm sorry for doubting you," she said, clinging to his lips, breathing shallow.

"I'm sorry for making you doubt my desire for you," he returned. "Do you trust me?"

"Yes. More than anyone in the world."

His gaze gleamed with satisfaction. *"Bene."*

When she thought he'd release her, he pulled her hands behind her, his scruffy cheek rubbing against her own. "Is that okay?" he whispered at her ear.

She was so lost in those dark eyes and his heated whispers that it took her a second to figure out he'd tied her hands behind her with the ripped shirt. Breath shallowing, she wriggled her wrists to find it was a very loose knot. The action made her thrust up her chest, and the sudden swamping heat on her skin told her she was bare to his intense eyes except for her lacy thong. Her nipples instantly puckered and goose bumps rose on her flesh. She let out a groan, unable to catch it.

"Cristo, bella. You're beautiful," he said in simple words, but his tone said so much more that for the first time in her life, Monica loved being in her own skin. "Every inch of you is…gloriously made."

And then he shocked her yet again by bending down and rubbing his scruff against her nipple. Arching her spine, Monica fell into the rough slide with a deep groan. One hand on her upper back, he held her still for his tender assault that continued to her other breast, her belly and then back up. Just when she thought she might grow hoarse with begging, he used his fingers and his lips and oh, God…his teeth.

Nipping and licking and suckling, he turned her into a writhing mass of sensation and pleasure. And then he moved down with his deliciously rough stubble and his wicked fingers and his decadent lips.

His filthy curse when he ripped the thong off her pinged over her skin; his scruff at her inner thigh made her writhe. The dig of his teeth at the fold where her hip met her thigh made her sob. His rough inhale at the top of her pubic bone, telling her that her scent was divine... She thrashed wildly to get rid of the knot. "Shh...*bella*, you said you would trust me, *si*?"

His pupils were blown and with his nostrils flaring and his mouth damp, she knew this was an Andrea that she would never forget. She nodded.

He pinched her nipple between his fingers and said, "Good girl."

A wealth of dampness bloomed between her thighs. And slowly, holding her gaze, he dipped his finger into her core and let out another filthy curse. Then he laved her wetness over her folds, tracing them with as much care as a cartographer charting new territory. "I want to taste you, Monica. Will you let me?"

Fresh tingles broke out against her skin as she stared at him. "I've never..." She flushed and tried again. "No one's ever done that and I..."

"If you don't want me to—"

"No, I do. I... You don't understand, that is, I'm not saying this well and..."

He waited, with infinite patience it seemed, while his palms dragged all over her trembling flesh as if he couldn't stop touching her. At least, that was what she told herself. And that gave her enough courage to see this through without mentioning what else was new for her. "I want to do everything with you."

"Good girl," he whispered again and with his words and kisses and caresses, he built her up into a frenzy all over again. Monica lost count of the times she thought she would splinter apart only for him to take away his hands and kiss her softly, tenderly, until she was not standing any longer at the edge. Over and over.

"Please, Andrea, I can't take this anymore. Please, make me come," she said, sounding both angry and begging. Her skin felt hot and damp, and she needed release so badly that she was close to sobbing. After all this time, after all the men who had called her frigid and boring and worse names, here she was, ready to sell her soul for an orgasm.

"Since you asked so well, *mia cara*." His hands on her hips, he pushed her up the bed.

Monica slithered over the sheets, every inch of her eager to do his bidding. Then he was kissing her belly again and lower and lower, his hands pushing her knees apart scandalously wide.

Her thigh muscles trembled violently when he finally, finally, bent his head and licked at her folds. The shock of that quick, rough swipe had her arching her hips off the bed, chasing his mouth shamelessly. And he did it again and again, setting a rhythm to which her entire pulse seemed to beat. "I need words, *bella*. I need to know what you need more of, where you want me deeper and longer," came his command in such gravelly tones that even that fueled her ascent.

So Monica told him, more voluble than she'd ever been when it came to intimacy; more abandoned than she'd ever been with another person; more demanding and brazen and alive and selfish than she'd ever been her entire life.

She told him she could take another finger after he thrust two inside her; she told him she was seeing stars when he hit some wildly responsive spot deep inside her, and she told him that she was *so, so* close that she couldn't think or talk or maybe even breathe. She told him she'd never felt like this with another man and she told him that all she could see and feel and know was his mouth and his fingers and his breath whispering over her folds.

His fingers pumped with a delicious rhythm that pushed her on and on, and his lips drew on her clit with a subtle tug…and her climax broke through, thrashing her about into so many jagged pieces.

Tears pooled and spilled at the acute, unbearable ripples jerking through her pelvis and down even as her hips still chased that wicked mouth with a mindless greed. Finally, his mouth stilled. She was desperate to touch him as he kissed a soft trail up her body, praising her, telling her how much he wanted to feel her fall apart around his cock, and she fell back against the bed, feeling wrung out and yet already thrumming with fresh need.

She slowly came back to herself as he undid the knot at her wrists, and it felt like she'd returned not quite the same. Which was ridiculous because it was one orgasm—albeit, yes, the kind that she'd heard friends and colleagues rave about. Her throat felt raw with all the screaming she'd done, and her limbs felt as if they were filled of thick honey, and her heart still hadn't returned to its normal pace.

When Andrea climbed up over into the bed, she instantly turned her face into the sheets, loath to reveal how much the orgasm had knocked out of her, physically and emotionally. God, he'd think her an idiot of the first order if he saw her tears. She pressed her face into the sweat-damp sheets, wiping away the wetness, feeling a sudden, strange shyness.

She rifled through one thing after the other that came to her lips, second-and third-guessing what she should say to break the building awkwardness, how she could speak to sound more confident and less…turned inside out.

"Are you okay, *cara*?" he inquired softly, one hand rifling through her hair with a tenderness she wouldn't have expected of him in a thousand years.

"More than okay," she said, sounding half-feverish, half-delirious. She couldn't blurt out how much she liked that he was still touching her.

It took her a few seconds, wrapped as she was in her own head, to realize that behind her Andrea had stilled. Except for those two fingers that moved over the scar on her waist with a compulsiveness that betrayed his usual indifference to most things.

"You really don't like that scar," she said, her tease sounding raspy.

"I don't like what it reminds me of," he said and then exhaled roughly.

Something about his tone made her desperate to see his expression. She jerked back on the bed, slipping and sliding on the now cooling sheets, to get a better look at him. Whatever teasing words she'd thought up disappeared because this intimacy was a punch to her gut. As much as the knowledge that he'd blasted through her defenses on more than one level.

Heat rushed to her cheeks as she met that dark gaze, the scene of just moments ago replaying in Technicolor in her mind. How she'd screamed; how she'd begged when he'd slowed down the pace; how she'd clamped her thighs around his head…and now the sight of those thin, sculpted lips that had woven such wicked pleasure through her.

"I know you know this, but she feels no lingering trauma from it," she said. Mentioning his mother when she was naked should have felt awkward. But it didn't. But then their relationship, if she could call it that, so far hadn't followed any rules or conventions.

He took a long while to answer, his brows furrowed, his fingers still dancing over the scar. When he finally spoke, his mouth was flat with tension. "And you think that's all that matters? That *she* is unhurt and trauma-free?"

Monica stilled, a cavern of longing opening up inside her.

He cared about her, in his own grumpy you're-another-nuisance-I-have-to-look-after way. She had known that even before the whole episode with Francesco. But to hear it in his words, delivered with that grumpiness, made her chest expand like some secret hidden chamber had been opened. She covered his hand with hers. "I'm unhurt, too, Andrea. And here, with you. Like this," she said, feeling the need to stretch and work loose the tightness in certain places. "And I know you will call me silly and pathetic and even twisted, maybe, but I met you and Flora and Romeo that day because of that accident, and you gave me a new life, and friends and almost-family, when I had nothing. And even without gaining all that, I would—"

"You would save Mama, I know, *bella*. You have little regard for your own safety."

"Not true," she said, inching closer and closer, pushing his shirt off his shoulders. "I know what I want and how I want it and I'm finally, thanks to you, beginning to flex my claws." She rubbed the tip of her nose against his with a giggle, and that he allowed this…was a gift, too. "I just don't stomp about, declaring and announcing and demanding that the world bend to my will and my wishes, that's all."

"Ahh…but in your case, I would make the bending to my wishes so worth it."

"Then what are you waiting for?" she whispered, finally taking his mouth like she wanted to, reaching for this man who seemed to have somehow tunneled deep into her heart without her knowledge.

He was an explosion in her mouth as she poured every ounce of need she felt into it. Her kiss lacked finesse but was filled with a new frenzy she didn't hide. He grunted into her mouth when she bit his lower lip, knowing already that he liked it a little rough, and she smiled, joy beating like a live pulse through her.

She gave in to all the overwhelming impulses, turned and stretched out like a lazy cat, and heard another rewarding grunt as her breasts rubbed against his bare chest. Flexing her newfound freedom, she sank into the stretch, while attached to him from chest to feet. The press of his thick shaft against her lower belly fanned out into a thousand flickers of fresh want and a near-painful ache where his fingers had been.

Leaning forward, she kissed his chin, and the sharp slashes of his cheekbones, and his thick brows and the scar that stretched out from his right temple to his mouth and lower. She trailed her mouth down to his throat and the notch there, across his chest and back up. Insatiable when it came to touching him, she registered the catch and release of his breath when she moved her mouth to the slab of his abdomen, those grunts and curses that flew from his mouth like punctuation marks to his pleasure. And it drove her on as she undid the trousers and pushed them down his hips. When his cock plopped into her palm, she pressed her thighs together and rubbed in a wanton gesture that did nothing to assuage her need.

She stroked him, slowly at first, marveling at the texture and shape and weight of him, and imagining how he would feel moving inside her; how he would submerge her in sensation; how he would own every inch of her dreams and wants.

His grunts and commands finally came to her past the deafening beat in her ears, and she squeezed him as he ordered her to, rubbed her thumb over the soft head, and when pre-cum pooled at the tip, she bent her head and licked at it without his command. It was strange and musky-tasting, and Monica needed another taste so she dipped her head again and closed her lips around his length.

It was uncomfortable at first, his girth stretching her mouth, but God, the rough, guttural grunts that fell from his mouth, and his fingers tugging at her scalp as if he was trying his best not to push her down and the instinctive thrust of his hips upward until he hit the roof of her mouth… It was the most daring and rewarding thing she'd ever done in her life.

She released him for a breath and took him in again, this time actually sucking a little more of him inside her mouth and laughing when he cursed, which turned into a hum when he filled her, which resulted in him telling her that she was such a "good girl" and *Cristo*, who knew her innocent countenance could carry such filthy spirit, and Monica wanted to stay in that moment forever and ever.

Two seconds later, she was on her back and heard the rip of a condom wrapper and he was lodged between her legs. Monica squeezed her inner thighs and her core muscles tight as if she could forever keep his hardness there, just there, where she needed it so desperately. One hand in her scalp tugged her head back, his lips playing and nibbling at her nipples, his hard hips bearing her down into the bed, and all that feverish longing she thought had been satiated came flooding back into her body.

Monica pressed up into him, arching into his touch when his lips moved up her neck, biting and licking and nipping, as if he meant to leave marks on her for days to come.

"I need you. Are you ready for me, *bella*?" he asked, and she nodded, feeling frantic and frenzied enough to burst out of her skin.

"Words, Monica," he said, his own breaths rough now, his thick shaft rubbing against her drenched folds. "Give me words and I will give you everything you crave, *bella*, and a little more that you won't ask for."

"I want you, Andrea," she whispered, pushing her face into his throat with a craven possessiveness she shouldn't feel, breathing the words into his skin, wishing she could keep the furor she felt from creeping into her tone and not caring at the same time. She bit his neck and pulled that pulse between her lips like he had done to her, and she felt the rewarding pressure of his body increase. "Like I've never wanted anything else in the world." It was her truth and she felt a freedom in releasing it to this man who had broken through all her known and unknown defenses.

She could feel his smile in his kiss and even that sliver of arrogance only heightened her feel of him, her experience of everything he gave her. She gasped as he pushed her knee into her chest and then he was there, testing her readiness again with his fingers, probing slowly before he moved inside her with one smooth thrust until he was lodged all the way inside.

"*Cristo, cara.* You will be the death of me," he murmured, hard and still around and inside her, his hands gripping her hips.

A pinch of pain speared through her pelvis, freezing her for a second. She dug her stubby nails into his shoulders with a stubborn possessiveness, holding his rising body as her anchor until it passed. And it passed soon, thank God, submerged by a host of other, new sensations. Quickly enough that she could marvel at the feeling of utter fullness of having him inside her. Fast enough that she could feel those thick tendrils of pleasure uncurl all over again as Andrea pulled out, almost all the way, and thrust back in. If he wasn't holding her captive with his lean, powerful frame, she'd have flown off the bed at the force of his thrust.

Monica bit her lip to stifle the moan that wanted to

escape. His teeth dug into her shoulder and his free hand pinched her nipple and he was stroking in and out of her as if they'd never been apart at all, and it was such a symphony of sensations that she thought she might pass out for a second at all the different layers.

"Monica, speak, *bella*," he said, twisting his hips in some strange dance that stirred that spot inside her again. Every time he did it, pleasure unfurled in a thousand new filaments, as if she was lighting up from inside out. "Tell me you're okay."

She cleared her throat, but still her words came out as if from a deep, dark tunnel where words didn't matter. Only sensations and pleasure and a strange sense of… belonging. One instance of good sex and God, she was ready to build a damned nest. "You ask for the impossible even here. Expecting me to talk right now is…unfair."

"Shall we push you off again, *bella*?"

Monica hid her face in his throat and whispered, "I don't know if I can. Just please, don't stop what you're doing. Andrea…don't stop."

His mouth found hers and Monica lost herself in the kiss and in the rough slide of his hair-roughened chest over her sensitized breasts. Then, somehow, he notched his thumb at her clit and every time he stroked in and out of her, he hit that spot inside her and soon, she was climbing that mindless cliff again, desperate for release.

Her orgasm broke through her like a shock wave, out of nowhere, and Monica screamed at the near-violent intensity of it.

She heard his filthy curse as her muscles milked his shaft and soon, there was a new intensity to his thrusts. Monica closed her eyes and her awareness hit a new plane with the sounds of his body thrusting into her, and his guttural grunts and the scent of his sweat and cologne. When she opened her mouth, she could taste his sweat, and then he was shuddering and shaking and she wrapped her arms around him as he pinned her hips into the bed with his and gave a hoarse shout.

Their breaths were rough and harsh-sounding in the sudden silence, the air scented with sex, and he was a delicious weight on top of her, and Monica knew she would not forget this moment if she lived to be a hundred.

CHAPTER TEN

WHEN ANDREA WOKE from the likes of a deep sleep he hadn't known in years, the light in the room was so bright that he had to blink a few times. One glance at his watch told him it was past ten-thirty in the morning.

With a groan, he fell back against the bedsheets, a strange lethargy stealing over his body and his head. With a languorous laziness he rarely indulged in, he reached out with his arm before he turned to his side, only to find the bed empty and cold. Which meant she had been up for hours.

He'd appreciated that in his assistant, but not so much in his lover. He also could just imagine those feathery brows of hers tying into a tiny frown, while she hesitated to ask him how she would know which role she was playing on a given morning. A silly grin stole over his face.

Whatever dissonance he had expected didn't come, and Andrea decided not to overthink it. If last night was anything to go by, their chemistry was off the charts and he knew very well it was the kind one didn't come by often.

What was wrong with enjoying it? With exploring the undeniable heat between them? Who said they couldn't part as he did with his other lovers? Yes, Monica was different, but she had gotten over her engagement with that rascal, hadn't she? Even better, she'd openly admitted to wanting Andrea, to dreaming of him.

It wasn't like she didn't know the ways of the world. More important was the fact that she knew *him*. Better than most women, better than even his family maybe.

And yet, there was something that had niggled at the back of his mind last night when his body had been sated. The surfeit of pleasure had numbed his thinking cells for a while. But it was something he'd wanted to ask her at the peak of his explosive climax.

Two minutes after he'd untangled himself from her so that he didn't crush her and inquired if she was okay, she'd disappeared into the bathroom, claiming she needed it. Laughing, he'd put it down to her shyness and then wondered at when he'd last laughed after sex. Usually, he was angry with himself for giving in to the temptation of sex when he had nothing else to offer, even though he made it clear up front to his partners, and then he itched to leave to avoid awkwardness.

It wasn't the way he'd been once. He'd had more than his share of lovers and girlfriends as a handsome, vibrant race-car driver with the world at his feet, but he had liked companionship, too. He had liked spending time with his then current girlfriend, or Chiara later, liked the connection and laughter it brought into his life.

Having grown up with parents who kissed each other at the drop of a hat and danced in the kitchen at the slightest chance and expressed their affection in that easy, simple way, had made Romeo and him grow up with the same need to form deep connections.

After the accident, everything had changed. Or rather,

he'd forced himself to change, to survive. But now, for the first time in years, he found himself wanting more than just a quick screw as some kind of stress relief. He wanted lazy mornings and long, glorious nights with Monica, and he decided he would enjoy every bit of it, as long as it lasted. He would treat her well, that was a given, but he would also indulge himself.

Once they had to break the engagement, which would be many months down the line, he would go back to his usual punishingly rigorous schedule at work again. With his body satiated and his mind resolved to the plan, thick sleep had claimed him. He had no idea how long she'd been gone because he had drifted off into sleep soon, still wearing a smile on his face.

He'd woken up in the hours of dawn to use the bathroom and found her at the edge of the bed, dressed in his shirt again, scrunched into a tight ball with her knees tucked into her chest, as if she meant to occupy the smallest space possible on the bed.

What she had shared with him struck him hard enough that Andrea found himself sitting at the foot of the bed, watching her sleep. She'd grown up in an orphanage first and then foster homes, had fended off wandering eyes and arms, had always dressed to minimize her looks and not to draw unwanted attention… Something he didn't want to feel or examine cracked open in his chest.

All the softer emotions that he had turned off, like tenderness and caring about anyone other than Mama and Romeo, cauterized for so long that he simply didn't feel them anymore, now pushed through like tiny new buds. He refused to let them send him into any kind of panic, though. At heart and by nurture, he had always been a man who cared about the people who revolved around his life, especially the ones who had less security, less privilege, in their lives. This…concern was that, that was all. As much as he chastised her for that sense of obligation she was forever mentioning, he felt it toward her, too.

How could he not, for the woman who had saved his mother's life? He and Romeo had nearly shattered at Papa's loss, so he could not even imagine their state if Mama had been hurt.

So yes, he would always "care" a little about this particular woman. Maybe even after they burnt out this chemistry.

When he had gotten back to bed, he had dragged her to the middle of it, to find her toes and fingers icy cold. The moment he turned her to face him, she came awake with a start and instantly stiffened, her arm coming up to block him. His heart had twisted in his chest, and his throat had felt thick with raw anger. Startled yellow eyes met his, fear slipping through the deep flush of sleep. "It's me, *bella*. You're safe," he'd said, running his hands through her long hair, kissing her temple.

In the next blink, she whispered something he couldn't catch, her body softened and with a tentativeness that tugged at his heart, she burrowed into him all the way. Her trust was a gift more precious than any he'd ever wanted or received.

With her face pushed up into his throat, her feet tucked between his legs and her curves tightly pressed against his hard muscles, all her stretching and wriggling had turned him rock hard. Hands stroking her back, Andrea had kissed her, urging her to wake up. It took all of five seconds for their kiss to turn voracious, their hands seeking and stroking, and when he touched her folds, she'd almost flinched. When he'd inquired, she'd admitted she was sore and two seconds later, drifted off into sleep again.

With that niggle narrowed down to a crystal-clear realization, Andrea shot out of the bed now. Pulling on sweatpants, he marched into the lounge to find her on the open terrace, her black agenda open in front of her on the table along with a cup of coffee and a bowl of fruit.

Dressed in a peach-colored sleeveless blouse with a V-neck and dark skinny jeans that looked like they'd been made to showcase her long legs, and her hair in a French braid, she looked like the prim and proper assistant she'd been for nearly three years. But he knew what lay underneath that simplicity and shyness, and he liked it way too much that he alone knew that.

"How long have you been awake?"

Monica startled so badly at that voice that she almost spilled the coffee on herself. At the last second, she let the cup slide onto the table and take the brunt of it. Only after she'd wiped the stickiness off her fingers and her heart resumed a relatively normal pace—she needed new normals around this man—did she turn her head.

Andrea was standing at the entrance to the terrace, dressed in loose sweatpants that hung low on his hips. His hair was a mess, his mouth was still swollen and there were deep, crescent-shaped marks right below his shoulder, thanks to her nails.

She flushed at the sight of him—with mortification but also with a visceral kind of satisfaction. Who knew she could be so possessive? Had all her instincts been lying dormant just waiting for the right man? What else would he unearth and unleash within her?

"Good morning," she finally managed, getting up from her seat. "You're out of the coffee beans you like but I ordered a different brand. I know you don't like change but you'll love this blend. I'll have a cup of coffee and your omelet ready, if you want to wash up and get dressed." With each word she uttered, he straightened from his relaxed pose and something she couldn't decipher dawned in his eyes. "I have also had the contracts sent over here from the legal department so that I can take a look at this new round of changes Mr. Brunetti's company is insisting on. I moved your appointment with Mr. Makiko to Tuesday, since you're visiting the manufacturing plant on Monday," she said, reading out the bullet points she'd marked on the agenda. "All the funds from yesterday's gala have been cleared and routed to the charity foundation's accountant. I have also had all your calls rerouted to me since I'll be taking over as your assistant again. Your temp is returning to the accounts department."

"Is that all?"

She shrugged and went to move past him. His fingers locked around her wrist, arresting her.

Monica shivered at the scent of his sun-warmed skin and the warmth from his bare chest and God, did he have to look so delicious first thing in the morning? Selfish wanton she was, she wished he would tug her closer so that she could soak in all of that heat from his body and kiss her senseless.

But he didn't do any of it. Instead, he released her once she stopped moving, his black-as-night gaze examining her face with an intensity she wasn't sure she could withstand without betraying herself.

Already, just the sight of him, disheveled and rough, had her body remembering the achy soreness she'd felt when she'd woken up, tangled around him. For long moments she'd stayed like that, her breath crashing through her as if she were a thief, intent on stealing something that didn't belong to her. He had been in such deep sleep that even when she'd untangled herself from him, he hadn't shaken.

Pushing herself up on her elbow, Monica had stared at him to her heart's content, tracing the scar on his face, the deep, jagged patchwork of scars she'd missed on his hip last night. In the end, her desperate need as she lay there for close to half an hour, watching him like some sort of lovesick fool, had made the decision for her. She wasn't going to cling to him or make any demands or even act like they'd done all the intimate things they'd done together. She would give him no reason for complaint, nor behave with even a whiff of lover-like expectations.

That was the only way this could work, the only way she could have him. So she'd done what she'd always done, put her head down and gone back to work, creating minimum ripples from him. She'd have even left the penthouse and given him space, if she could be sure her face wouldn't betray her night's activities to Romeo and Flora as if it were a high-def plasma television.

"Where did you get the clothes?" Andrea asked, startling her out of her reverie.

"I called the villa hoping to get Shania, Romeo's physio. Instead, I got Flora," she said, flushing.

His mouth twitched. "And?"

Monica sighed. "She made me give her a list of things I needed, packed all the things she made me buy at that boutique when she learned of our plans and told me she'd order two sets of toiletries, for here—" she moved her hand to indicate the penthouse "—and the villa because you don't know your own schedule and I want to be wherever you are, right?" By the time she had finished the retelling, his grin had deepened and Monica wanted to thump him for laughing at her embarrassment. "You know how Flora gets when she decides on something. I barely got in two words."

"Mama knowing about us bothers you. Why?"

"I don't want her to think I'm taking advantage of the situation, of you."

He laughed then, throwing his head back, drawing her attention to the column of his throat and his bobbing Adam's apple and his lean chest. Mortification swirling through her, Monica let out a filthy curse and instantly felt wrong for doing it.

Andrea's laughter doubled, and he had to bend down with his hands on his knees to balance himself. This time, when she went to pass him, muttering to herself, he not only stopped her again, but also lifted her in his arms, ignoring her rabbit-like squeal, walked into the lounge and sat down with her in his lap.

One arm wound around his neck, Monica drew in sharp breaths. An intense ribbon of longing held her in a chokehold as she stared at the deep grooves around his mouth. His eyes danced with mirth and she thought he had never looked more heartbreakingly gorgeous.

"I'm glad to provide entertainment for you. Maybe I should also add *clown* to all the roles I perform for you."

"Don't tempt me about performing for me, *bella*," he said, nuzzling under her jaw and drawing a straight line to her earlobe with his teeth. She shivered anew. "I might throw a list of bullet points for your agenda. Especially since I'm feeling deprived after waking up alone. You should have stayed in bed."

Monica arched into his touch, her nipples peaking painfully as his mouth drifted lower, tugging the V-neck of the blouse as far as it would allow. She hummed at the back of her throat, an action she didn't know she was capable of, begging him wordlessly to do more. His scruff was rougher than the previous night, and pleasure jolted down to her sex when he pushed her blouse and bra roughly down and rubbed it against her nipple.

It was decadent, wanton and felt so filthily divine that she thought she might come apart at the seams.

Moaning, writhing on his lap, she sank her fingers into his hair, keeping him there. He licked at the needy knot before drawing it into his mouth. Monica jerked at the swift pool of dampness that one action caused and God, if he continued, she would come just like that and… He stopped.

Then he was tugging her bra and blouse back into place while she trembled with unmet need. "You're dangerous, *bella*. That wasn't what I had in mind for this morning."

"Then why did you start it?" she asked, unable to keep her peevishness out of her tone. "You…you…"

Brow risen, Andrea watched her with a keen interest, the earlier amusement returning to his eyes.

She struggled to get off his lap but his arms were steel bands around her. "I'm beginning to think you find this all hilarious," she said, anger and something more beating at her. "Me, I mean."

"I find you...sweet and naive, *bella*," he said, the humor vanishing from his eyes. "But it doesn't mean I'm laughing at you."

The tenderness in his voice could undo her so easily. Monica nodded without looking at him. This time when she tried to stand, he let her go, and she wished she hadn't.

God, she was a contrary fool.

Instead of running away or clinging to him, she chose the middle ground and settled on the coffee table in front of him, her legs on the outside of his, pathetic enough to want that little bit of closeness.

Hand under her chin, Andrea lifted her head. His dark eyes searched hers, challenging her to hold his gaze. "Now, tell me what this morning is all about."

She wished she could lie or fob him off with some flirty remark, or have the guts to grab him and kiss the hell out of him like she wanted to. But she was who she was and Andrea wasn't someone she could deter when he set his mind to something. "I...didn't want to be a nuisance to you. And I didn't want you to think I was expecting anything. Work had piled up anyway so I thought I should just...make myself useful."

He nodded, looking thoughtful. "This doesn't have to be awkward, Monica. We're consenting adults who trust each other, *si*?"

"I just... I panicked because I didn't know how to behave in this context and—"

"Because you've never done this before?" he cut in.

"No," she said, this time managing the fake flirty smile. "I haven't had a red-hot affair with my boss before."

"No, you've never had sex before."

Her gaze met his and her silence offered its own answer without her permission. Suddenly, she understood the intent behind his frown before. If he called her pathetic again…she might get actually mad and stomp out of there. "I think that's my business."

He leaned forward, trapping her between his thighs before she could pull away again. "I agree, *bella*. I only wish you'd told me so—"

"So you could find another reason to put me off? I don't know about you but I truly enjoyed what happened last night, Andrea. And I have zero regrets. Maybe this is about you and your—"

He caught her mouth in a devastating kiss that would have taken her out at the knees if she hadn't been sitting. There was none of the gentleness from last night, no exploration, no building to something more. Only rough, hard possession, making her words a lie, making her tingle from head to toe, telling her in no uncertain terms that this was a two-way obsession. At least for now.

His tongue plundered her mouth; his teeth nipped her lips as if in punishment for her doubts and God, his hands stroked over her hips and her back and sank into her hair and tugged her neat little braid until she tilted her head up in complete surrender. "I have plans for this braid and you." His words sent pulses of damp desire arrowing down to her core. Like a bow, he pulled her body taut and tight under his hold, ready to splinter at one tug. And she didn't mind one bit.

All her life, she'd hidden in the margins, making safe, defensive choices, always toeing the line of security but now, she was more than willing to let it all unravel at his hands.

His mouth left a wet, hot trail down her blouse, and then he bit the curve of her breast. "Still believe I didn't enjoy last night?"

Hands splayed on his thighs, she scooted closer and closer until somehow, she was on his lap and his erection was notched right where she needed it. She cursed herself for wearing skin-tight jeans. "Let's leave it at that, then."

Slowly, he released his hold and pulled back. This time, Monica couldn't help it, she ran her thumb over his lower lip and farther down until she could trace the marks she'd left on his skin. God, she loved touching him like this, loved knowing what he liked, just…knowing him at this intimate level.

"You were engaged to that scoundrel, *cara mia*. I'm trying to understand what was going on and if I need to find him and thrash him."

"I know how…it looks and I want to share some things with you. But what if it makes you laugh at me?"

His mouth flattened with quick anger and she felt stupid for projecting her own insecurities at him. "I'm not him, *bella*."

"I know that. I didn't mean to…"

"It's okay," Andrea said, covering her mouth with one finger. "You're from such a different background than me. And so young and…" He shook his head as if he couldn't be *that* honest with her. "I would never laugh at anything you've done to survive in this world, ever. In fact, I think you are a marvel, *bella*, to retain that spirit of yours after such a start in life."

Every word of his took down some unknown brick wall she'd built around herself, made her feel seen. And until now, she hadn't known how much she needed someone to see it, someone to tell her that she had survived it all without losing parts of herself. And that it was this man who had her trust, filled her with a giddy kind of joy, with a rightness that she felt down to her marrow.

Monica leaned into his chest and wrapped her arms around him, tears beckoning at the backs of her eyes again. And then while she hid her face in his throat, she talked, because she'd always wanted to talk to someone about it all and who better than this man who somehow made her brave enough and bold enough to reach for her deepest desires.

"When I was growing up, I... My body developed too soon," she said, the past swirling through her mind like a movie. "By fourteen, I was as tall as I am now and I had this face and these breasts and these legs but no one to help me understand why I seemed to draw the worst kind of attention from boys and men. Maybe if I had continued to live with Father D'Souza, he would have explained it to me, but he wasn't allowed to have children older than eleven."

Andrea was stiff beneath her, his fingers cradling her scalp, his other hand stroking down her body as if he meant to make the telling easier. "Father D'Souza?"

"I was left as an infant on the steps of his church. He's like a...father to me, the only family I've known. When I was old enough, I decided I would take his last name."

"That is the man you visit every year in New York."

She smiled, remembering how cranky Andrea had been last year when she'd been gone for three weeks. "Yes. He worries about me and I worry about him. He's seventy-three now and I like to see him at least once a year. My aptitude for languages... He recognized it first, encouraged me to take courses at the community college. He was also the one who urged me to go on a vacation the first time I came here, helped me with the funds even. Now he keeps asking me if I'll ever move back."

"What do you say to that?"

Monica hid her grin. She didn't miss the stiffness of Andrea's tone when he asked that. "I tell him that I'm building a good life here, that I have friends and a grumpy boss who will probably hound me across the pond if I take off for too long. He was worried that first year, after the accident." She instantly regretted going there as Andrea's hand stilled, but pushed on. "But now he knows about all of you. Romeo and he have an ongoing online chess game, even."

"Send a donation to the orphanage in Papa's name," he said, that ring of command back in his voice.

Monica hid her smile in his chest. As his personal assistant, and sometimes Flora's companion at these events, she knew how many charities Valentini Luxury Goods supported. But this particular donation...meant a lot to her. Even bracing herself for him to laugh at her, she kissed his cheek and whispered her thanks.

"I'm sorry for interrupting you. Tell me more about... you."

She refused to examine why it was so easy to pick up where she had left off, why it felt so good to tell him things she'd never admitted to anyone, even Romeo, who had become a true friend.

Was it the protectiveness that Andrea gave off? Or just simple, abiding trust in him? Or was it the fact that he was the man who had helped her push through the armor she'd built around her own sexuality? Or was it all of it?

"It didn't take me long to realize that my looks, my own body, was a curse. I shied away from anything that remotely touched on my femininity or my sexuality. There was another guy when I was eighteen. He wasn't unkind, but I couldn't get out of my head. When push came to shove, I…backed out. I realized I wasn't really into it. With Francesco, we…kissed and did other stuff. I tried so hard but I just couldn't go all the way. He was frustrated and I was frustrated. I wanted him and me to work so much. I had this perfect life in my head and he suited it to a tee. He said we had all our lives and it was another reason why I fell for him. I thought he was so sweet to wait, ready to try again. When I reached him after he dumped me—" Andrea's arms tightened around her waist "—he said I was a shiny package but the contents were useless or something like that. That I was like a cold, hollow sculpture, useful only for showing off."

"He needs to be taught a lesson," Andrea bit out.

"He's taught me one thing, though, and I'm grateful for that."

"Forgive me if I don't ask you what that is, *bella*. You're far too forgiving and generous to attribute any good thing to him."

Monica clasped his cheek, feeling the most insane urge to hug him, which was definitely not a sexual urge. A part of her marveled that she could touch him freely like this, could talk to him so openly, while the other part of her was wary to flex her newfound role.

She settled for a soft kiss on his lips, pouring out all these new sensations fluttering through her as if a thousand butterflies had been released. Gratitude and more fluttered on her lips but she didn't dare try to put it into words. She wasn't sure what would come out.

"What was that for?" he asked, raising his brows.

For a man who rarely showed emotion or liked it in others, he was very good at reading her and her kisses. She shrugged and before it could get awkward—or was it her own wariness at this kind of intimacy?—she stood up and checked her watch. "We do have a few matters to get through today."

"What a strict assistant you are, *bella*. It is Saturday."

"And you have worked every Saturday since I joined the company."

"Today I feel like goofing off. I will spend the day in bed with my fake fiancée and explore her very real passion. There are a few things I didn't get to try last night. So, if you can see yourself out for the weekend and call her in, *por favor*. I'm eager to get started."

How had Monica not known that it was possible to blush and smile at the same time? Where had he hidden this flirty, roguish side of him?

He was already larger than life but to see this real side of him… What woman could stand a chance against him? She was beginning to feel like she was on a ride that only went up and around, making her dizzy. Biting her lower lip, she took a step away from the sitting lounge. "Your fake fiancée is busy today."

"Busy with what?" he said, standing up, every inch

the arrogant CEO who wanted the world arranged just so at his command.

"She's going to a pizza- and gelato-making class."

"With whom?" he prompted, coming unerringly to the point.

Monica considered evading for one moment, and then sighed. "Romeo. We made the date weeks ago. I can't cancel it because you've decided you want to…stay in bed. The chef is like a genius and his classes take months to get in and the gelato is to die for. After the last few weeks… it's the one fun thing I've been looking forward to."

"I would never want to stand in the way of your fun, Monica," he said, taking a step in her direction. "Only, you will go with me instead of my brother. He hogs too much of your time anyway."

"I like spending time with him. And I'm not ditching him just so…" Her words fell away as he began stalking her across the open layout, a wicked twinkle in his eyes.

"Just so I can indulge us both, so I can taste you again? Just so I can give you a bullet-pointed agenda for the day's activities and see how fast we can get through them all? Your efficiency does drive me wild, *bella*."

She blushed and he was laughing and Monica thought she might burst apart at the seams. Desire and anticipation, yes, but this easy joy… God, it was like magic, vibrating through her every cell. "You really want to take the Saturday off and make gelato with me?" she asked, disbelief punctuating her words.

"With you, yes," he said, catching her. And then his mouth was on hers and Monica forgot about mergers and charity funds and gelato, and maybe even the reason for breathing.

CHAPTER ELEVEN

LIFE MOVED AT an insane pace for Monica over the next two months as Andrea's novelty fiancée. And she definitely was a novelty, she realized with increasing wariness.

For his family, because Andrea seemed to play the role of a possessive, protective fiancé with an easy aplomb they hadn't expected. More than once, she'd seen a shadow pass across Flora's eyes but the older woman, sweet as ever, never gave voice to whatever doubts she had. Thankfully, neither did she ask Monica much about their "fake relationship," treating her with the same kindness as always, and that was enough for her.

For his friends, colleagues and extended family, all of whom orbited Andrea for some sort of help, she was the "poor orphaned American woman" who had caught Andrea's fancy. *Temporarily* was implied but not said. Most of them, though, were smart enough to play nice with her since she did have his ear. The smart ones even understood that she not only knew every big business matter that passed his desk but that he also trusted her.

More than once, their casual attitude toward using his wealth and reach for their own benefit, as if he owed them that due to his meteoric success, rankled Monica.

There were one or two people who wanted his friendship for no other reason than that he was a dynamic, witty person to be around. But Andrea did not allow that closeness.

One of them was her earlier boss, the CFO for Valentini Luxury Goods. While he trusted Maria, Andrea kept it purely professional with her, even though Maria had known him for years.

For the rest of the world and the media, she was a novelty because, once they had decided to believe Andrea's version, their affair was nothing short of a fairy tale coming true.

Having never spent a moment as the center of attention at any stage of her life, Monica struggled with it at every party and gala and public event, where she was cast as the beautiful American upstart of unknown origins, the woman who had stolen the gorgeous, powerful bachelor that all of Milan adored. Wherever she went, on Andrea's arm or with Flora and Romeo, she was besieged with questions about their relationship, as if they wanted to decipher how she had landed the uncatchable Andrea Valentini.

But for every second that she cringed at the invasive questions, flinched at camera flashes going off in their faces and tried to hide behind Andrea's broad frame like a scared rabbit, she enjoyed the glimpse she was getting into how fun and charming and utterly seductive he could be.

Romeo kept reminding her that the fake engagement suited his brother, that she was good for him, that he hadn't seen Andrea this lively and fun in a long time. Monica tried not to let it go to her head, though there was more than a grain of truth to Romeo's assessment. Hijacking her gelato-making date had been only the start.

She blushed profusely even now, remembering how Andrea had surprised her that evening when they had arrived at the world-class restaurant kitchen. It had been only them and the chef. All the other participants had been highly compensated to attend a different session, because Andrea Valentini wanted to learn how to make gelato with his media-shy fiancée in private, and the world had better arrange itself accordingly. For once, his high-handedness and his refusal to parade them in front of an audience had worked out for her.

It had been one of the best evenings of her life. From the sheer pleasure of spending hours in Andrea's company—his lips and hands constantly touching her in a hundred little ways, as if he couldn't help himself—to how he'd distracted her with whispered promises that her tiny batch of gelato had turned out awful while his had been mouthwateringly perfect, and the end of the night where they had barely made it back to his penthouse, full of delicious pizza and gelato and wine, and he had taken her against the wall just barely inside the elevator.

Even then, he'd first made sure she wasn't still sore, with his fingers. When it had been clear she was just as eager as him, he had picked her up, held her against the wall, pulled her sundress up and thrust into her with one hard stroke that had had her banging her head against the wall.

It had been fervent, frantic, near-frenzied, how they'd clawed at each other.

And in the weeks since that night, their frenzy had nowhere near calmed. Not hers, and definitely not his.

Monica almost wished their fake relationship only centered around the very real passion and chemistry that seemed to imbue every touch and caress. Then she could have firmly told her increasingly invested heart to stay out of the whole matter. She wanted to believe that at some point in her life, she would have met a man who would have disabused her of her hang-ups and fears about her body and her sexuality. Because she'd weaved them all into place to protect herself against a harsh world. She wanted to convince herself that that man just happened to be her boss, whom she'd trusted beyond any other man she'd ever met.

Andrea, at every turn, proved all the things she tried to tell herself to be lies.

It wasn't just the phenomenal sex or the incendiary chemistry between them that made Monica feel as if her life was simultaneously rushing fast like a river rapid and grounding to a halt like the rich earth under.

Because there were moments where it seemed, impossibly, marvelously, that he cared about her, that he enjoyed her company as much as her body and her kisses and her wild, deep need for him that drove him to his own edge.

That, however, was a slippery slope of wishful thinking because she wanted to truly live her life this time, take each day as it came with Andrea, however many she got, instead of making it fit into some childhood template of a dream life.

What she really wanted was to take initiative in their personal life. Not that she had a problem with following whatever Andrea decided—in the two months of their roller-coaster, fake and yet somehow real relationship, she had done more fun, adventurous things, had laughed more, had explored her own sexuality at his patient hands, had understood her own needs and wishes better than ever before.

She had lived in these two months more than she had her entire life. And she wanted to believe that it was the same for him, too.

He did seem livelier and more relaxed, more prone to spontaneity and taking time off work, since she'd resumed working for him. Still, wary reluctance was a knot in her belly anytime she wanted to cross a line that really wasn't there. So when that particular day approached that Andrea would not work, Monica ensured his schedule was clear and made plans to make herself scarce.

It was the day more than a decade ago when they had lost their father. Everyone, even at work, knew that Andrea disappeared that day. Not even Romeo or Flora knew where he went or how he spent it. As his new assistant two years ago, Monica herself had been witness to the change in his demeanor even a week ahead of that day each year, of how the shadow of grief ravaged him.

But…a small part of her desperately wanted to talk to him this time. To spend it with him, even if in utter silence. To provide a little solace and companionship to him on a day when he retreated from the world, and even his family.

She was still mulling over how she could do it without crossing a boundary when Andrea entered and closed the door to the office behind him. Monica looked away from her screen and rubbed at her gritty-feeling eyes.

It was eight in the evening on a Wednesday and the

glittering lights of Milan's financial district shone through the floor-to-ceiling glass walls of Andrea's office.

They had been going through the final corrections that the legal department had sent on the merger with Mr. Brunetti's company since six in the morning. Not only was Monica bone tired after being up until two for a dinner with Andrea's business associates, but she was also worried about him.

All day, words had formed and dusted away on her lips as she waited to see signs of his mood spiraling or retreating. Instead, he had been on a high the past two days. Mr. Brunetti had finally agreed to most of Andrea's terms for the merger, and they had been working hard and playing harder. He'd been relentlessly demanding in bed, and Monica had begun to wonder if sex could be used as a way to blunt painful reminders of grief. Not that she minded one bit being used like that…

A file plopped onto the coffee table in front of her.

"You missed two pages of corrections again," Andrea said, planting himself onto the table.

Embarrassment flushed her cheeks as Monica opened the file, found the pages he was referring to. "I'm sorry, there's no excuse." Foolish, useless tears formed a lump in her throat. How could she have missed it? God, she prided herself on her work and this was unacceptable. "I'll look through these and get the new changes entered immediately. You'll have them ASAP."

When she made to get up, he leaned forward, his legs straddling hers and locking her in place. "That's two times you made a mistake today. And two times in the three and a half years since you started working at this company."

Monica looked up to find his eyes full of that sardonic humor. And that spark touched her heart as if it were a warm tendril wrapping around the chamber, cocooning her from the world. Slowly, she straightened her spine, when all she wanted to do was to lean into his warm body and let him envelop her. "That's two times too many for my liking," she said, flipping through the file. "I don't know how it happened but I promise you that it won't happen again, and—"

"It happened because I've been working you too hard," Andrea said, taking the file from her hands. He leaned in where she had pulled back and rubbed the pad of his thumb under her eyes. "You look exhausted, *cara*. Why didn't you tell me you needed a break?"

"*You* didn't take one," she said, drawing a finger across the gaunt brackets around his mouth. God, how she loved touching him like this, as if he was hers to do so. And what was she going to do when this merger was all signed off on? When his interest in her and the necessity of this fake relationship began to dwindle? How would she keep her hands to herself and her thoughts free of him? How would she sit across from him in this same office and pretend like she didn't want more of him?

Her thoughts looped in the same way, even as she tried to detach herself from them, detach herself from this growing feeling that pervaded every one of her waking and sleeping moments.

"You have double standards here," she said, smiling to make the complaint seem shallow. "Even Romeo agrees that you never slow down, despite preaching it to him."

"My fiancée and my brother are going behind my back and discussing me?"

"We're too afraid to say it to your face," she said, wondering when he'd begun to drop the fake part from her title. She tried so hard to not read anything into it.

"I have spent years training my body and my head to survive on little sleep and rest. For you, though, it has been long nights and long days, *si*?" His gaze encompassed her entire body, from her hair in a loose bun to her tight dress shirt and her black trousers, lighting every inch of her on slow, deep fire. "I should have realized I'm making too many demands on you. Which is something Mama and Romeo have been hounding me about."

"I like spending time with you. At work or outside of it. I mean, yes, I could do a little less of all the socializing and networking dinners as your fiancée but all the rest, I like it, Andrea. I like what we do together," she said, and then blushed so hard that she had no doubt her cheeks must look like tomatoes.

"I like how intensely you admit that, *bella*," he said with a grin and caught her mouth in a whisper-kiss that made her heart thud against her rib cage. He tasted of coffee and mint and like decadent want, his mouth drawing her deeper with each nip and stroke.

She kept waiting to see if the raw need she felt for him would dial down or change with each kiss and caress. But it hadn't. It didn't. If anything, now she craved him like a drug that she needed to function fully in the world. His kisses and his teasing and his carnal demands in bed… She reveled in every moment, yes, but now they were tinged with a deeper emotion, carried more weight with each passing day.

Like every single time, their kiss rose to a fever pitch soon, tinged with a desperate need on both their sides, racing toward more. Maybe because it had been a whole thirty-six hours since they had made love. They had been so busy last night that they had fallen into exhausted sleep as soon as they had returned to his penthouse.

She protested with a mewl when Andrea pulled away, even as her fingers were locked against his nape, holding him to her. Her eyes closed as he swept his mouth over her jaw and that sensitive spot where her neck met her shoulder. Shamelessly, she thrust herself into his touch, and had the even better reward of hearing his laughter.

Finally, he pulled back from her again, and she was glad to see his own pupils blown up with desire and more. There was always a little more that tinged his desire, too, but she could never be sure if it was only what she *wanted* to see.

His mouth trailed upward and landed at her temple, his rough fingers circling her nape with a possessive protectiveness that she'd longed for her whole life. "Go home, take a shower, catch some sleep and then I want you to take a couple of days off. There's a little mountain resort within two hours that the chauffeur will drive you to. I'll join you tomorrow night."

"No," she said, something close to panic rising within her. They couldn't go off this weekend, of all weekends. When he realized what it was, he would hate her. "I need to finalize these documents and—"

"I've been pursuing this merger for more than two years. Brunetti has thrown every obstacle in its way and we have resolved them all to our satisfaction. Signing on the dotted line can wait for a few days."

"It's not just work I'm worried about."

"Whatever is on the social calendar, cancel it. Why the

resistance, *bella*?" He drew back, as if to search her face for some hidden meaning. Something she'd never heard before underlined his words when he spoke. "Aren't you the one forever nagging me to take it slow for just a little bit?"

Her cheeks heated at that word. "No, nothing on the social calendar. I already cleared the rest of your week, beginning tomorrow. I knew you wouldn't want to work on Friday and…"

"What's Friday?"

"It's the…twenty-third of September. You…usually don't work that day."

He reared back from her so fast that it was like whiplash. He had forgotten the significance of the date, she realized with a belated sort of horror, and that was exactly what was reflected in his face now.

He looked horrified that he had forgotten. And fast on the heels of that came guilt that filled his eyes.

Monica stood up, wanting to follow him, some knot of fear and guilt trapped in her throat making it hard to breathe. He walked away from the sitting lounge, his moments lacking that economic grace that made him a pleasure to watch. When he reached his desk, he rubbed a hand over his face, his shoulders tight with tension.

"Andrea, it's a small oversight. We've been busy with this merger and you——"

"I do not need you to assuage my guilt, Monica," he said, without turning around. But she saw his reflection in the windows and how he rubbed the heels of his palms against his eyes. It was a rare gesture of vulnerability that he never showed the world, not even his family. And definitely not her.

Monica, he'd called her. Not *bella* or *cara mia*. And in that particular tone that he rarely used anymore. She swallowed the sliver of hurt it invoked. This wasn't about her or their relationship. But somehow, she couldn't swallow that lie. "I'd never tell you to feel one way or another, Andrea. Just as you can't tell me to not care about you."

Her words landed in between them, creating a minefield she couldn't cross without it exploding in her face.

"I do not need your care. Definitely not in this and not in any area of my personal life. I thought you understood that."

She nodded even though he couldn't see her and rallied herself into acting as if the vast room wasn't suddenly swathed in tension. Gathering her files and folders, she started stuffing them into her laptop bag. "What you suggested earlier is a good idea. A weekend at the resort, I mean. I'll make arrangements for your stay. Anything that comes up, I can manage easily."

"What a thoughtful assistant and lover you are, *bella*, easily shifting from one role to the other, not making any demands in either," he said now, turning around, his mouth wreathed in a cynical twist he rarely showed her anymore. It was almost as if the Andrea from those beginning years of their acquaintance was back, and she was nothing but one of his dutiful sheep.

"I'm thinking of you," she said, a reckless kind of boldness sweeping through her. "I know you don't let anyone, not even Flora or Romeo, do that, but I do. And I won't apologize for it."

"And yet, you're not insisting on accompanying me on the trip."

"Not this time, no," she said, each step she took toward him feeling like an obstacle course she was jumping over. "I have a feeling anything I suggest will only rile you up right now."

"What a good little rule follower you are, always weighing your risks."

His words landed like a punch to her gut, given they carried so much truth in them. That he would taunt her for what she thought was her weakness...hurt on so many levels. "You're...not in a good place now and I have no problem being your target," she said, anger coming to her aid. "But don't presume to know how I feel or what I want."

"Tell me what you want, then," he said, the words full of some craven demand. "Tell me what the perfect assistant, perfect lover, perfect fake fiancée, Monica D'Souza, truly wants."

"I want to go to the chalet with you. I want to be with you and give you the space to talk about anything and everything. I want to give you companionable silence. I want to go to bed with you. I want you to tell me about that awful day. I want you to not struggle with your grief alone. I want to hear about what kind of man your father was, in your own words, because I know he must have been amazing to have raised you and Romeo to be who you are. I want to watch over you as you do for everyone that comes into your sphere. I want you to be not alone because every moment you are, I'll be thinking of you."

His gaze lost the dark humor, icing her out. His chin reared down as if she'd attacked him instead of offering a short respite from his grief and his guilt. "I don't need to talk about it, *bella*. There's no big emotional resolution I'll achieve by talking about how I drove Papa into crashing our car. There's no big breakthrough I'll get by talking about how Romeo almost died because of my selfishness. There's nothing you can do that will change that day and what it stole from me. Or what it turned me into," he said, turning away. "You're one of a kind, *bella*, I'll give you that. But you cannot change me. And if you're beginning to think that…"

"Oh, don't worry, Andrea. That kind of arrogance has never been my strength. As for wanting to change you or claim you…even I'm not that naive. But—"

"I think you should leave. Before I say something I cannot take back."

Monica had known this was coming, this clearly drawn line in the sand that would shove her back beyond that boundary. Her entire life had been about lines like this that told her she was wanted only if it was convenient, only if she behaved well, only if a foster family was faring well financially, only if she behaved perfectly, only, only, only…

Something that had been forever yoked to that fear, that she might have a family or love if only she stayed behind that line and didn't ask much, splintered. Suddenly, it felt as if she had been set free from a huge weight and it was both terrifying and liberating.

With that came a kind of recklessness, even as she dutifully walked back to the other side of the line. She had a question to ask. And it flew from her mouth like a bullet. "Are you angry that for the first time in a decade, you were so happy with your own life that you forgot the relentless grief you carry as some kind of shroud? Or are you angry that it is our fake relationship that made you forget? Or is it that you have decided you cannot be happy at all?"

His shoulders tightened enough for her to know that her question had landed exactly as she'd intended it to. But she didn't wait for his answer because Andrea Valentini was an honorable man and she didn't want to make a liar out of him. Though there was little satisfaction in knowing she was right.

Her heart felt heavy in her chest as she walked out of his office and closed the door, even as every inch of her wanted to stay, wanted to be strong enough to withstand his misdirected anger and guilt and hold his hand through the pain that came later.

CHAPTER TWELVE

IT WAS A full two days before Monica returned to his family home, a huge bunch of wild lilies clutched in her hand. The moment she saw him, wariness turned the corners of her lush mouth down.

Andrea had spent the anniversary of his father's death mulling over the questions she had posed for him and chastising himself for being hard on the one person who had dared only to think of him. He still didn't know what to think or how to process the fact that he had forgotten that date this year.

For years, it had stood out like a black mark against his very soul on the calendar, reacquainting him with guilt and grief and raw pain that he took on as punishment. He spent it drinking, replaying the argument with Papa, regrets piling up until he couldn't breathe. For days, he would be unable to face Mama or Romeo for fear of seeing their hatred or resentment or even grief. He had never allowed himself the luxury of grieving with them, of reflecting on what they'd all lost that day. He'd forced himself to be alone, both as punishment and repentance.

And yet this year, all that had changed.

She had changed it, even as he had taunted her that their relationship didn't matter in the scheme of things.

Not a minute after she'd left, he'd regretted his callous words. Still, he was cowardly enough not to want to face her even though her hurt weighed on him like another shroud. He didn't have an answer for her question and was ruthless enough to know that he wouldn't give it to her even if he had it.

Instead, he had turned up at his family home two mornings later, so that it wouldn't look like he was seeking her out. Neither did he miss it that she had drawn him here on that day when he'd stayed away for so long. Only she wasn't there and instead of the heavy silence he'd braced himself for, he'd heard laughter, the kind that surged up from one's belly, like a cleansing fire.

He had shocked Mama and Romeo in the middle of watching those home videos Papa had made out of every tiny occasion, their laughter ringing around Romeo's high-tech studio lounge.

Transfixed by the sight of the laughing man in the grainy video on the screen, Andrea had folded himself down onto the sofa, a little distance away from them. Papa had come alive for those videos, dancing with Mama while he or Romeo held the camera precariously, playing with them, teasing them…

They had watched those videos for hours, laughing and shouting and reminiscing and at the end, Andrea had found his eyes wet and his head achy and his heart somehow lighter and yet heavy, too. Mama had buried her face in his chest and sobbed silently, even as she hurried to reassure him that she loved him with all her heart. That whatever his father had dreamed of for him and Romeo for the future, he had fulfilled it a thousand times over and wouldn't he forgive himself, too?

And Andrea had realized what a fool he'd been all these years. How unnecessarily he'd suffered through his grief alone. On the heels of the first came another realization. He didn't want that life anymore, where he punished himself, where he struggled alone, where he hid himself from his family. It was the exact opposite of what Papa had wanted for his firstborn.

Beneath all of it was the gnawing realization that two days had passed since their argument and Monica still hadn't returned. Only Romeo's admission that she'd told him she was fine and needed space had stopped him from calling the *chief commissario* of the police to look for her.

The third morning, she walked into his home, her pale pink sundress rumpled—had she slept in it?—and an expensive bunch of wild lilies, her favorite flowers, in hand. Her mouth instantly drew down when she spied him prowling the garden around the patio. Her hair in a messy braid, her eyes wearing that haunted look he'd seen once before—the very sight of her made emotions surge through him. Gritting his teeth, he sought control, trying to find some rationality out of the thorny knots.

He had worried over her safety. He had…hated sleeping by himself and had repeatedly reached out an arm, desperate for her warm body across his bed. He had… missed her with a longing he couldn't kill or define. And with each hour that had passed, he had become more determined to come up with a plan that would both satisfy his needs and prune the buds of things he didn't want to feel or nurture.

Seeing her, hearing his heart thud in his chest and his body tighten with desire, told him this was the change he sought in his life.

Turning their fake engagement into a real one was a simple and brilliant solution. Monica would have what she'd wanted all her life—family, security and a promise of a long, solid future. If she wished, they could even have children.

He would have her in his bed, and when passion waned as it eventually would, they would have a stable partnership built on loyalty and friendship and mutual care. It wouldn't be the soulless business merger with Chiara, but neither would it be the great love story his parents had shared that had left his mother shattered. It would be something in between, something that suited him and Monica.

She knew him, maybe better than anyone, and she would understand what a reach this was for him, would know how far he was willing to go for her. *Just her.*

With each second, the idea held more and more appeal. She would be his. Her loyalty, her generosity, her affection, her passion, her days and nights, all of them would be his. The very thought sent a staccato of urgent need beating through him.

"Where the hell have you been?" he asked as she skated a wide arc around him to reach his mother and Romeo, who were breakfasting on the patio.

She kissed Mama's cheek and then wrapped her arms around Romeo from behind, smiled when he whispered something in her ear and then planted a sound kiss on his scruffy cheek.

Bitter jealousy ran rivulets through Andrea, tying his stomach in tight knots, and he swore to himself that he would have that easy affection from her, too. He'd never been a patient man and now that he knew what he wanted, he wanted it sealed and done now. He wanted her acceptance now. He wanted to tell his mother to plan the wedding so that they could have it as soon as possible. Then he would whisk her away on a short honeymoon— with this merger going through, he could afford at least a weekend. And then he would punish her, in the best way he knew, for this stubborn act. For cutting him off for two whole days, for being unavailable to him when he'd been desperate for her. He would give her so much pleasure that she'd never even think of parting from him again.

After what felt like an eternity, she turned to him, her chin lifting at that stubborn angle that both infuriated him and fascinated him no end. "Good morning to you. too, Andrea. I have been staying with a friend, taking a break as you ordered me to."

He walked toward the breakfast table, not liking the reminder that she had sought his brother for help, yet again. To avoid him specifically. "You switched off your phone."

"I wasn't working and you told me to steer clear of you." Her eyes held his, and at whatever she saw there, she sighed. "Romeo knew I was fine."

"What about what you owe me?" he bit out, not hiding his frustration, and her eyes widened. "Was that your little petty punishment because I behaved like an ass? Because it worked."

Whatever anger and defiance she'd drummed up seemed to drain out of her at his admission. Her hand shook as she lifted the carafe and poured a cup of coffee, added a spoon of cream, stirred it in and handed it to him. Even now, she catered to his wishes and unspoken needs first and damned if he knew how to feel about it.

He was shocked enough to grumpily say, "I don't need your peace offering." But the scent of her was already working on him, making his body buzz.

"I know you worry over me, and you think I'm some naive lamb out in the jungle. If I try really hard—" her mouth twitched "—I can even appreciate where your concern stems from. But it's not necessary."

"I disagree."

She thrust the coffee cup into his hand and went back to the table. Loath as he was to have this spat in front of his mother and Romeo, he settled down at the table. They'd been pestering him about their "little fight" for days now and this way, they would understand his intentions and he wouldn't have to reassure them that he wasn't hurting their little lamb.

"What's with the flowers?" he asked after taking a few sips of his coffee. Already, his day felt better, in his control, with her seated across from him and his plan cementing in his mind.

She ran a finger over one fragile petal, shying her gaze away from his before she said, "Birthday flowers from Francesco."

Silence fell over the table. Even Mama's look for Monica was full of soft chastisement.

"That's the friend you've been staying with?" Andrea bit out, jealousy clinging to his throat like a thousand tiny pinpricks. "Did you run to him the minute we fought?"

Her head jerked up, her gaze blazing with fire. *Cristo*, why was he saying all the wrong things? "If you really think that—"

"I don't." He rubbed a hand over his face, wondering what the hell was wrong with him.

"I stayed with that waitress friend of Romeo's," she said, cutting his brother a cheeky grin. That grin should be his, as should the light in her eyes. "We went to the lakefront in Navigli, and Francesco was there with some friends. He came over, ordered expensive wine, remembered all of a sudden that it was my birthday and bought the flowers from one of those expensive shops. He was trying to show off his elevated life status and it was easier to accept them than argue with him."

Another regret to add to his mounting pile, Andrea thought.

It had been her birthday and he'd sent her off to spend it with strangers, by herself. And that scoundrel knew that little detail about her and he hadn't. For the first time in his life, Andrea wished he could redo the whole past few days all over again.

Mama broke the spiraling tension between them. "Four years and you didn't tell us the same day is your birthday, Monica? We would have celebrated it with you!"

Monica shook her head, dislodging a thick strand of hair from her braid. Andrea felt the most overwhelming urge to tuck it behind her ear and pull her into his lap until she poured down all the reasons for her swollen eyes and pinched mouth. If it wasn't just him, that is.

"I know how hard that day is for you all. As for my birthday, I don't think it's even real. It was the day Father D'Souza found me on the front steps of the church. We simply decided that would be my birthday."

"Giovanni would have been delighted to know that the anniversary of his death could be marked with celebrating such a lovely person like you, *cara mia*," his mother said, her words trembling, but her mouth stretching into a wide smile.

"We will celebrate it tonight," Andrea said, and his mother and Romeo added their excitement.

Monica stared at him, her hand stilling on her own coffee cup. Anger flashed in her eyes and yet, she pushed it away with the sort of control he'd never seen her possess.

Andrea sat back in his chair and watched her, his gut tight with some strange sort of premonition. There was something different about her, he realized, even though she'd only been gone two days. Like a wall of newly erected defense between her and him. Like she wasn't being herself.

When she looked at him, her gaze was calm. It was not the Monica he had known for almost four years, the woman who wore all her emotions like bright colored signals on her face. "Is it okay if I excuse myself, Flora? I want to shower and maybe catch up on some sleep. I'm afraid I don't feel good."

When his mother nodded, she stood up and left without so much as blinking in his direction. Effectively dismissing him, which was novel in itself.

Bemusement and something more sang through Andrea's veins. He'd never seen her anger or her armor before and he didn't like it one bit employed against him. Especially the latter.

He followed her slender frame up the stairs with his hungry gaze. Disappointment curdled through him when she chose to go to the room she had convalesced in, instead of his suite where they'd been staying for the past two months.

"I believe the Americans call it being in the dog-house," Romeo supplied softly, unhelpful as ever.

"It was her birthday and you forced her to spend it with a stranger. You better make it up to her, Andrea," his mother said, casting a shrewd glance at him. "If, however, you're bored with her, it might be better to tell her. I do hope you know that I will not be picking sides."

"Hardly, Mama," Andrea said, reaching for her hand and giving it a squeeze. "For once, you're going to be not only impressed with how I plan to make it up to her, but thoroughly ecstatic."

Her eyes widened and even Romeo looked stunned for once. Andrea kissed her cheek and left for his own shower, ignoring his brother's rapid-fire questions. He'd let her sleep a little and then he'd make it up to her.

Monica came awake slowly, and instantly sought her cell phone to check the time. Instead, she found the electronic alarm clock that rested near Andrea's bed winking at her, the red digits showing it was just past six. Frowning, she sat up in the vast bed, the luxury cotton duvet clinging to her bare legs, the all too familiar navy furnishings and that cozy scent of wood shavings making her body react as if it were a scent specifically designed to comfort and arouse her in equal measures.

"Feeling better after your nap?"

She turned to find Andrea sitting at his woodwork-ing desk, torso bare and whittling away at a small slab of dark ebony wood in front of him. For a few moments, she simply watched his fingers use tiny tools with the same precision he used against her intimate folds. Heat flushed within her at remembered pleasure.

He wasn't even looking at her yet somehow knew the exact moment she'd woken up. Closing her tired eyes, she told herself to stop reading meaning into the silliest things. Especially now, in a vulnerable state after the phone call she'd received this morning from one of the two friends she'd made at the orphanage about Father D'Souza.

It was not good news and yet, somehow it felt like if it had to happen, it had happened at the right time. Somehow, even in his ill health, the kind father was looking out for her well-being.

Pressing the heels of her thumbs into her eyes, Monica willed the roiling panic to abate. She knew what she had to do. All weekend she'd wondered how she could shore up her defenses against him, how to finish this thing between them with dignity instead of letting the coming end consume her.

Fate had handed her a way out and now, all she had to do was act on it. And yet, there had been something different about him this morning. He'd shown more emotion—yes, it was masked by jealousy, but it had been there. Even a sense of urgency. It had taken all her willpower to run from him, though she knew she needed the reprieve.

The bed dipped at her side the same moment a wall of warmth rubbed up against her arm. She felt his fingers on her cheek, the abrasive pad of his thumb tracing her jawline. Her breath came in deep, eager pants, the scent of his sweat and soap making her nearly delirious with desire and longing. "Monica? I was an ass to you in the office, *bella*. Forgive me." He whispered the words into her temple, one arm coming up behind her to hold her loosely.

Monica leaned her side into his chest, automatically seeking whatever he would give. "Forgiven," she whispered, hiding her face in his neck. God, he smelled delicious, and she wanted to burrow under his skin.

His fingers encircled the nape of her neck, the tips digging into her scalp, and she pushed into the touch, needing that rough, fierce claiming of his. Her nipples drew into tight, painful points under her flimsy tank top at first contact with his hard chest.

She rubbed herself against him, like an animal in heat, and licked at the hollow of his throat. Usually, she didn't even do that much. In two months of their relationship, it was always Andrea who initiated touching, kissing and playing. The few times that they had sex without any foreplay, it was because they'd engaged in it indirectly for hours on a hectic workday or at a party with little, intimate touches or sitting across from each other at his mother's table while Romeo called them lust birds.

Always, it was he who reached for her and always, Monica was more than willing and ready for him. But today he gently but firmly pushed her away and she felt a sudden flash of anger. She'd spent two months making sure she never asked him for more than he was willing to give, never even going near the boundary he kept around himself. Except two days ago. And now again…

Turning stiff in his arms, she tried to jerk away and off the bed.

He didn't let her. His fingers trapped her wrists and tugged—with that ever-present gentleness he always showed her—until she was prostrate against the head-board and she had no choice but to look up at him.

"I have something important to say to you," he said, bringing her palm to his cheek and rubbing against it. He was kneeling between her thighs, and her world was reduced to this gorgeous, possessive man and his gloriously warm body. How was she supposed to walk away from this?

"I'm not in the mood for talking."

"You're always in the mood for talking, *bella*."

"Well, not right now. I want something else. And if you won't give it to me, I…"

He raised a brow. His mouth twitched but there was an unnerving intensity to his gaze that she'd never seen, that arrested the juvenile taunt she'd have thrown at him. Flushing with heat and something more, she said, "If you don't want to give me what I want, just say so."

"When did I ever deny you anything you asked for, *bella*? Truly asked for?"

Dismay curled through her as his gaze held hers. He was right. Even that day in his office, she'd given him a rhetorical answer with a lot of "woulds." She hadn't demanded to go with him. But it was also only true because she'd never made any demands of him. And today, on the day when she had to make the hardest decision of her life, she did want something from him. She wanted *him*.

She scooted closer to him. Pushing him back onto his haunches, she straddled him until his shaft was pure torment against her core. "I want to have sex, Andrea. Now. I need you inside me. Please," she added, her gaze flitting between his eyes.

"As you wish, *bella*," he said, catching her mouth

in a brutally tender kiss. She was on her back on her next breath and he rocked his erection into her core, his tongue plunging into her mouth with the same erotic insistence.

Monica clung to him like a rag doll as he got rid of her tank top, leaving her in her silk panties. Then his mouth drew a line down her neck, between her breasts, and he played with them just how she liked, kneading and cupping, his tongue and teeth leaving marks on her. With a loud groan, she tugged at his hair roughly when he wouldn't touch her where she needed it and finally, finally, his tongue circled her nipple and his lips drew the tight knot into his warm mouth and Monica bucked off the bed.

His rough stubble against the sensitive nipple made her shout his name in a brazen demand that she'd have blushed at any other time. But more than just desire beat through her. Was it brushed with a stroke of grief and pain at what she was losing? Was it loss if she never had it in the first place?

Urgency beat through her veins, a desperate need to bottle everything from this moment so that it would last her a lifetime. And for the first time in their relationship, she didn't want to passively wait for him.

When his fingers dipped into her folds and stroked her clit in those mind-numbing circles she liked, it took her everything to jackknife herself into a sitting position and push at his chest. "I want to touch you," she announced.

He catered to her with a wicked smile and shifted to lean back against the headboard, lacing his hands behind his head. Licking her lips, Monica tugged at his sweatpants and he lifted his hips until they got rid of them. Then holding his gaze, she wrapped her fingers around his cock.

Arousal thrummed through her as if it were his fingers touching her intimately, instead of the opposite. He was all thick hardness wrapped in soft, velvet-like skin here, the exact opposite of the man he was everywhere else. Already, she could see the tightness around his mouth, hear the rough grunts of his breaths, feel the infinitesimal thrust of his hips when she stroked her fist all the way to the base and then up, until she was squeezing the soft head. "Monica, look at me," he said, his words a gravelly whisper that slid along her skin like pings of electricity. "You don't have to do everything today, *bella*."

"I want to, Andrea. I want to taste you and suck…" Here, she blushed beetroot red, no doubt. "And do all that stuff that men want their lovers to do. I want you to…come inside my mouth, or on my face or wherever you want to. I want to make your filthiest fantasies come true. I want to be everything you need."

His hands circled her nape, bringing her up to him so his mouth could take hers in a rough, hard kiss that told stories of his actual wishes. "We have time for you to do all this, *bella*. And you're already everything I want."

Tears pooled in her eyes as those simple words speared through her with the force of a silken thrust. Those were the words she wanted to hear, but in a different context. Her stupid, stupid heart. "I want to do it now," she said on a thready whisper.

Leaning down, she licked at the soft head and before he could recover with a curse and a grunt, she opened her mouth and sucked him in. He was salty and musky and he stretched her mouth too wide but God, the sounds he made, the filthy curses that fell from his lips, the "good girl, just like that," he kept saying, made the little discomfort worth every inch of it.

Monica followed his instructions to the letter, and could feel his body draw tighter, his hips thrust up when he lost control, his erection hitting the roof of her mouth, his need to go deeper and harder, his thighs rock hard against her nails.

His fingers tightened in her scalp, rougher than ever before, a breath before he was pushing her back into the mattress and with one rough stroke that almost pushed her off the bed, he entered her.

The sensation of being claimed by him like this… It was the most connected she'd felt to her body, to the world around her, and yet somehow, utterly divine, as if her soul couldn't remain untouched. A lone tear escaped her and fled into the bedsheets.

"I was rough. *Cristo*, did I hurt you?"

Monica licked her lower lip and shook her head. "No. It was…perfect. As it always is. But I want more, please. I want you to move. I want you to make me forget. I want…so much, Andrea, and it feels like I will never have enough of you." She looked away, scared that she had said too much, betrayed her innermost feelings somehow, even though she hadn't even articulated them for herself yet. She braced for him to push off or withdraw or even to just finish what she'd demanded he give her without acknowledging her mindless words.

But as always, Andrea surprised her.

Whatever he saw in her face, or heard in her words, he gave her more than she asked for this time. Hands under her hips, he pulled her up until she was in his lap, straddling him, entrenching him even deeper inside her.

Throwing her head back, wrapping her arms around his neck, Monica let out a deep groan. "God, it feels like you're everywhere inside me like this."

"Look at me, *cara mia*," he said against her mouth, and she complied.

Fire burned in his gaze as he trailed tiny butterfly kisses over her face.

And then he was thrusting up into her and Monica knew she'd never forget this moment. Sex in this position was different, raw, on a visceral level. They were joined head to pelvis and she felt as if she was enveloped in this gorgeous, generous man's very essence. With every upward thrust of his, she bore down until they found a rhythm that reverberated with their heartbeats. Her breasts pushed against his chest and when he dragged her hand to her clit and said, "Come for me, *bella*," she felt a new, wild, wanton heat thrash through her.

Touching herself while he watched her dialed up her pleasure another notch. It was filthy and awakening and when her fingers wandered down and touched the place where he thrust in and out of her, he let out the filthiest curse of all, and as his gaze told her he was almost there, Monica fell apart. Her orgasm ripped through her out of the blue, with the force of a wave pulling her under, and then there was nothing but swimming through the hazy pleasure of it while Andrea's thrusts became rougher and wilder and his body pressed her down into the bed when his own climax claimed him.

Their breaths were a rough, harsh symphony in the sudden silence, their bodies damp and sweaty. And then when he pulled back and kissed her temple and whispered, "Marry me, Monica," it felt like fate had dealt her the cruelest hand one more time. Only this time, it was couched in the shape of her deepest, darkest want.

CHAPTER THIRTEEN

SHE SAID NOTHING in reply for so long that Andrea began to wonder if she'd heard him at all. Through the long, hot shower he carried her to, through the sudden foray into the kitchen in their robes when her stomach growled violently, through their return to his bedroom—giggling, after Flora had found them in the kitchen and watched them with red streaking her own cheeks—to feeding each other bits of cheese and figs and grapes and washing it down with wine. Through another bout of sex after Monica had demanded to know one of his fantasies and he had bent her over the arm of the couch while they watched each other in the full-length mirror. He began to wonder if he had said it at all.

Even wondering that, Andrea had fallen into a sort of blissful sleep, wrapped around her, after two days of emotional turmoil. When he suddenly startled awake, dawn was streaking the sky with fingers of pink, and the side where Monica slept was not only empty but cold, too. Again.

He shot to his feet, pulled on his sweatpants and followed her voice into the closet to find her packing her suitcase with her cell phone clutched to her ear.

He lasted two minutes before he grabbed the phone,

ended the call without checking who it was and threw it behind him until it clanged against the floor with a loud thud. "Why are you packing?"

"You brute! That was my phone."

Hands on his hips, he gathered all the patience he could find within himself. There was a strange flutter in his chest, like a panicked bird beating its wings. "Why are you packing, Monica?"

"I have to leave," she said, shying away from his gaze, folding a sweater.

Shocked beyond reason, he grabbed her wrist, gentling his hold as he always did, and pulled her behind him back to the bedroom. He turned all the lights on and was struck by the sight of her anew. Deep shadows cradled her eyes as she wrapped her arms around herself. She looked as if she hadn't slept a wink. Andrea ran a hand over his face, willing his anger to cool, his spiraling emotions to plateau.

"Leave for where, *bella*? And why are you packing at dawn, like some thief stealing away before morning hits?"

"I wasn't going to leave without saying goodbye. The airline called about my ticket and I thought I might as well finish packing."

"Again, why are you leaving? To where?" he said, knowing that he sounded like a desperate child and not caring.

"A friend told me that Father D'Souza has developed pneumonia. He has no one to look after him. I need to do that. I want to. For once in my life, I'm in a position to give my time and energy to him. I can't leave him alone in this condition."

Relief shuddered through him, even though Andrea felt awful for the old man. This was a solvable problem. This was within his control. "I will have a nurse by his side within the hour. He will not be alone," he said, immediately reaching for his phone.

"Yes, but that would be a stranger. Not someone he knows."

"*Bene.* You can go in a couple of weeks, then. I'll even accompany you. You can spend a couple of days with him, making sure he has everything he needs and we can make a trip out of it. You always tell me how much you love New York in winter. It could even be our honeymoon trip."

Her shoulders sagged but her head jerked up. Her gaze widened. She swayed where she stood like a leaf in a storm. "You're joking."

"Twice in a row about something like this? You know me better than that, *bella*," he said, grabbing her hand. He felt this…strange, almost desperate, overwhelming need to touch her, to hold her, to anchor her to him in every way possible. He didn't question the urge.

Seating himself at the edge of the bed, he pulled her to him. And something in him calmed when she came without the protest he was expecting and buried her face in his chest. She was trembling, he realized, and tightened his hold. Her arms went around his waist, as if she was intending to vine herself around him for days to come and yet, she was planning the opposite. Lifting her chin, he kissed her and all the urgency of the past few days came rushing back. A thread of something curled within him, roping tighter and tighter around his chest.

When he pulled away, she mewled in protest. He dug

his fingers into her hair and pulled her head until she was looking into his eyes. "Tomorrow. We will get married tomorrow. Mama won't like it but she'll be too happy to—"

"Why do you want to marry me?" she said, eyes wide and emotions slamming through them one after the other. There was hope and excitement but also doubt and confusion and some new inner resolve he didn't know how to break.

At least he had an answer ready for this. "I like having you in my life. I like that I can trust you in every way and I like that you and I share the kind of passion that one doesn't come by often. I like knowing that I can give you the kind of security and family that you've always wanted and dreamed of. Is that not so?"

Tears filled her eyes and overflew, the tip of her nose turning adorably red. She swiped at the tears slowly, her gaze never leaving his. "I did. I do. But I... I want to be by Father D'Souza's side as soon as possible."

"That's not an answer, Monica."

"I can't think of this now, Andrea, and—"

He nodded. "We will fly with you to New York in a couple of days, then. Mama and Romeo and I. We can marry in that church with the father's blessing."

Her mouth fell on a gasp, and a smile cut through the tears. "You're serious."

"Of course, I am."

A groan seemed to wrench out of her and she mumbled, "You're making this so hard," while drenching his chest in fresh tears. Then with a deep breath, she stood, stepped back from the circle of his arms, the line of her shoulders stiffening. "You didn't like my disappearing on you for two whole days, did you?"

"No. But—"

"Marrying me is about efficiency for you. About keeping things in control. About compromise, *si*?"

"I have no need to marry you, *bella*. So what am I compromising on?"

"It's giving me just enough without truly letting me in," she said with an empty laugh and scrubbing at her cheeks. Even watery, her eyes shone with that resolve he'd never seen in her before. "My dreams are not the same as they were three years ago, a year ago or even three months ago when you saved me from Francesco."

"So you don't believe in marriage and family and security anymore?" he asked, unable to keep the taunt out of his voice.

"I do, and you have no idea how tempting your offer is. I'd have your trust and your fidelity and the security you offer and Flora's love and Romeo's companionship. I'd belong to you, like I've never been anyone's. But all of those things can't make up for the one thing I need. You have changed me, Andrea. Being with you these two months… It's unlike anything I'll ever live through again. It's taught me so much about myself."

"You talk as if you're…" His heart gave a swift kick against his rib cage as realization landed. He stood. "You're ending this. You came back yesterday with this intention set. You asked me to make love to you as some sort of wretched goodbye. All night, you laughed and talked and kissed me…with this in mind."

"I don't want to, but I have to. Before it gets ugly and I start clinging to you. Before you push me away again.

Before I do something that violates that boundary around yourself. Before my heart shatters into so many pieces at your feet. But more than anything, I need to understand what this is."

Every thought and word that came to Andrea was ugly in its shape and full of a bitter jealously. And after those came something worse. He felt as if he were in that floundering car again, yelling at his father to steer into the skid, yelling at Romeo to sit back, yelling and yelling and yelling until he could no more and the oncoming tree loomed larger and larger and fear shone in Papa's eyes and he was shouting, too, telling him that he loved him, asking him to look after his mother and Romeo, telling him that…and then there had been nothing.

Not sounds. Not sights. Not the tears in his father's eyes, or his moving lips, or his fingers' death-like hold on Andrea's hand. Nothing but wretched darkness consuming him. And when he'd woken up days later, the world had been painfully colorful, so bright and yet so empty that he had wished himself to be swallowed up back into that darkness.

He had vowed to himself that he would never feel like that again. Never feel such love again that it left him searching for the dark. And yet, here he was, losing his foothold on reality again, losing something he had never wanted at all.

"Andrea, please try to understand," she said, reaching for his hand.

He jerked away from her, his action now one of self-preservation. Somehow, he made himself look at her. The large lamp behind her limned the contours of her face and body with loving care and he wondered at how empty this space would feel without her.

"I don't," he said, reaching for some composure. It didn't matter that he could see the pain in her eyes, in her entire body. All he could focus on was the sinking sensation in the pit of his stomach. "But it is your life and as you made it clear over the weekend, you owe me nothing."

"Is that what you truly think?" she asked, anger etching itself into her words. She looked impossibly, achingly beautiful then, her emotions making her bolder and taller and making her shine brighter than he'd ever seen her before. As if her very conviction was a light inside her. "If I told you I'm in love with you, would you still marry me? If I told you it hurt to be sent away from you, it hurt to not reach for you and offer solace, it nearly ripped me apart to know that you might never feel the same about me as I do you, would you still marry me? If I told you I'd settle for nothing less than love, would you still be ready to marry me?"

He would've been less shocked if she'd slapped him across the face out of nowhere. "You've imagined yourself in love before, Monica, and look how that turned out." The moment the words poured out of his mouth, he wanted to snatch them back. *Cristo*, what was the matter with him? Why did he always say the worst things when it came to her? Why did he hurt her when it was the last thing he wanted to do?

And he had his answer as surely as she let out a humorless chuckle. It was the very thing he'd always been determined not to feel, the very thing that was making him lash out at her, the very thing that was turning him inside out at the thought of losing her. But he could not give in, could not take that risk.

Her arms went around her middle, as if he had attacked her but she'd also expected it. It shamed him that she knew him better than he knew himself, that he had proved her right. "This is why I need to leave. I can't be near you, much less marry you when I feel this way. When I don't know if this is just me reaching for security again. When I don't know if these feelings that make me so angry at you can be trusted, when this constant knot of fear sits in my throat, warning me that I shouldn't ask for more, I shouldn't crave more, I shouldn't demand more than you give. I don't want to be in a relationship with that fear in my heart. I never should be in one unless I know I can ask for whatever I deserve. It's not fair to me. It's not…" She gasped in a pained breath. "I don't want to live in that fear. I don't want to love you with that niggling whisper in my heart. So I have to leave. I have to say goodbye to the best thing that has ever happened to me. I have to let go, even though I don't want to, and hope that in the future, I will know a love that doesn't come with conditions. I have to start believing that I deserve that kind of love. And *you* made me realize that, Andrea. Even if you can't offer it."

She came to him then and went on her toes and kissed his cheek and pressed her cheek to his chest, her arms going around him again, as if he was both the storm and the port and she was caught in the middle.

Andrea couldn't bear it. Couldn't bear to smell her and hold her, and touch her and kiss her, all the while knowing that she was leaving him, alone and adrift in the snow again.

He pushed her away from him and left the suite, wanting to be swallowed up by darkness again.

Andrea hadn't imagined, in his darkest nightmares, that he would feel her loss so keenly every single day.

Of course, the fact that Monica had run his life like a well-engineered machine, always anticipating his needs and meeting them before he even verbalized them, made it impossible for him not to miss her.

But it wasn't just his work life. It was the way she'd made him laugh; the way she'd dragged him along to every new experience that she was determined to have; the way she'd sit quietly with her knitting while he worked on his sculptures; the way she'd seemed to bring him back to the man he'd been once before.

Ever since the accident, he had drawn a boundary around himself; had reduced his life to a single dimension—work—and let everything else about him die a slow death. But that had never been what Papa had wanted. He had never asked Andrea to turn himself into a machine.

He had only asked him to be careful with his racing, to dial down the unnecessary risks he had begun to take, the highs he had started chasing, to think of others before himself. And yet, as punishment, Andrea had turned himself into another version Papa would have hated, too.

He would have told him that life was to be lived, with the ones you love, that one's heart was for more than just beating and pumping blood. He had shown him and Romeo by making their family name stand for so much, by loving their mother so well that to this day, that love was a shining light in her smile.

How could Andrea be anything less? What was left of his life without Monica? How was this empty darkness better than the light and laughter she had brought him?

The merger was done, production had started on the new plant and yet he felt no surge of pride or sense of satisfaction. All he wanted was to hear her voice one more time, see her and hold her.

He knew Romeo was in touch with her, but he refused to ask his brother about how she was faring. It was bad enough neither his mother nor Romeo would meet his eyes or say a word to his face. For all that she'd said she wouldn't take sides, Mama's displeasure was clear.

But as weeks piled into a month, what little pride he had hung on to had dissolved. For a few hours he decided he would fly to New York, to offer support to her while she tended to the man who had shown her kindness and love, without imposing any conditions. He wouldn't ask for anything, demand anything.

But then her face swam into his vision, her eyes full of anguish when he'd straight out told her that she'd believed herself in love before. *Cristo*, he'd been cruel to taunt her for what she thought was her weakness. Still, she'd behaved so bravely, *his fierce little mouse*, walking away from him, *from them*, from the golden future he'd painted using her darkest fear against her, to get clarity, to know herself, even as she'd told him she was in love with him.

I don't want to love you with that niggling whisper in my heart.

How could he then be any less brave? How could he chase her to New York and steal that time and space she'd asked for? How could he browbeat her into saying yes to him and then wonder for the rest of his life if she truly loved him?

Suddenly, he understood the anguish of the dilemma she'd faced.

If he truly loved her, which he realized he did painfully with each passing day that he didn't see her or touch her or kiss her or hold her, he would give her the space to figure it out.

He would let her be, let her know herself, see herself as he saw her, the vulnerable yet fierce, the generous but bold, the gentle but brave, creature that she was. He would wait and hope that when she did have that clarity that she would come back to him and give him just one more chance.

Just one chance and he would lay the world at her feet.

Every cell inside him revolted at the idea of waiting, of leaving the decision in her hands—at least for now. He balked at the idea of not chasing her down to wherever she was in the world and seducing her and kissing her and bending her to his will, at the idea of not making her say that she loved him all over again. He was not a man used to inaction, to letting others dictate his happiness and yet there was another thing he was coming to recognize—his happiness was with her.

In her kisses and embraces and her soft smiles.

It was the pain and uncertainty and the anguish that came with loving her, the very thing he'd wanted to avoid. But then he'd remember the sweetness of her kisses, her shy boldness when she was under him and looked up at him with those yellow eyes, and the soft, slow way she'd stroke his lips when he laughed, as if she wanted to bottle the sound. The easy, effortless way she had loved him, even when he hadn't been able to appreciate it. And he knew that it was all worth it. That without this pain, they would always be unsure of each other. That now, he could live with nothing but her unconditional surrender, and his own in return.

The waiting made each day that much longer, that much more unbearable. Whatever they saw in his face now melted Mama's and Romeo's silent admonishments.

Then suddenly, as he sat working on a wooden piece in his new shed that gave him little pleasure without her company, it came to him. He would give her the one thing, *the only thing*, she'd ever asked of him and hope that she'd understand his message.

That everything that was his, his mind, body and heart, were all hers, if only she'd demand it of him.

CHAPTER FOURTEEN

IT HAD BEEN three weeks since Monica had returned to Italy and joined Valentini Luxury Goods again as an executive assistant. Only instead of assisting the CEO, she was now working for the Executive Head of Design, which was Romeo. Working for him at his studio, where he allowed no one, and staying at his girlfriend's place, hadn't made Monica any less worried about running into Andrea. Or any less eager.

It felt unnecessarily sneaky, though, and Romeo wasn't happy about it. She didn't blame him. But the good friend he was, he also understood that she had needed to do this.

She'd spent two months looking after Father D'Souza and when he had not only recovered but also returned to his work at the orphanage as if he were a spring chicken instead of a seventy-three-year-old man, Monica had found herself not only heart-sick but at a loose end, as well. As much as she loved Father D'Souza and was glad to see him restored to his full self, her life wasn't in New York.

The new friends and family she'd made were all across the ocean. Even as she'd nursed Father D'Souza with full devotion, her mind, heart and soul had remained behind with *him*. Thinking of Andrea, remembering the look in his eyes when he'd asked her if she was ending it, the shock that seemed to reverberate through him when she'd proclaimed that she loved him, she hadn't been able to sleep or eat or function in any kind of normal way.

All she could think of was whether she'd made the wrong decision, if she'd thrown away a lifetime's worth of belonging and happiness by confusing her feelings. Not for one moment could she stop imagining what life would have been like if she'd said yes.

Would they have been married already? Would she have shown him all her favorite spots in New York? Would she have settled into married life as well as she'd settled into being his fake fiancée? Would there have been a day where she woke up and realized that she was simply another cog in his life, like everything else that was convenient and easy and suitable?

Would she have been happy knowing she loved him and he would never love her back?

When the last question came, she inevitably fell into the thinking she'd been right to leave, though it provided no solace.

But one thing had become clear.

She had to be strong enough to return to Italy because her friends and life were there. She was still connected to Flora and Romeo, still connected in some way to Andrea. She had to reclaim her life, her strength, in this way. She might even have to face a future where Andrea would move on with another woman and would simply have to hope that someday she might move on, too. Though at this point in time, it was impossible to think of a moment or a day when she wouldn't love Andrea with a soul-deep need. At least that much had become clear to her across oceans and two months of time.

So she'd returned to Italy, asking Romeo to help her find a job and start afresh. As much of a businessman as his brother, Romeo had said he was loath to let talent like hers go off to another company, especially with her familiarity of the company culture and organizational systems. Her first instinct had been to beg him to find her something else, but she knew she couldn't avoid Andrea forever, either.

She couldn't run and hide and avoid life, as she'd done for so many years.

And yesterday, another mundane, lifeless day in a number of them, it seemed, a small cardboard box had been sitting on her desk in Romeo's studio, looking a little worse for the wear. She realized why when she looked at the different stamps. The little package was addressed to her and had been sent to the orphanage, but must have missed her by days. Father D'Souza must have received it and forwarded it to her here.

Hands trembling, breath whistling through her as if she'd run a marathon, Monica pulled at the tape and the numerous layers of bubble wrap around the object. She was sobbing by the time she got the last one off and the little dark mermaid danced in her hand.

Through her blurry vision, she ran her fingers over the delicate contours of sculpture, marveled at his craft with wonder in her heart. And then she was unfurling the small note, torn out of his notepad, and read:

Ask me, bella. For whatever you want.

Her knees giving out under her, Monica had fallen to the floor, clutching the little mermaid to her chest, her heart expanding so big that it might explode out of her. He'd given her what she'd asked for. He'd always give her what she asked for, if only she was brave enough to ask for it.

So here she was at his family home, in the bedroom suite she'd shared with him, knowing that Romeo was out and Flora would be at her friend's anniversary party, wondering if her sudden burst of bravery had, after all, been a foolish idea. She didn't even know if he would be home tonight. But she'd wanted to surprise him and had even thought up an excuse in case he was in a frightful mood.

She was staring at the pieces on his desk, shocked at seeing several new ones, her throat full of that sticky pain she felt whenever she thought of him, when a voice said behind her, "Should I call the *polizia* on you, Ms. D'Souza?"

Monica whirled so fast that her head felt dizzy.

Andrea stood against his closed bedroom door, eyes alive with an unholy shine that sent a thrum of awareness through her. It was the look he got when he wanted to tease her, or torment her extra for her climax, or when he wanted sex. Basically, all the times when he wanted her, saw the real her, the American orphan that no one wanted.

He looked like he hadn't shaved in a couple of days but otherwise, he looked as magnetic and gorgeous as he had ever been. His dress shirt hung open to reveal the rough hair on his chest that she loved to touch, and the black trousers he wore emphasized the lean power of his thighs.

Meeting his gaze, though… She felt like every bit of

oxygen had been sucked from the room and she was almost lightheaded from the impact.

"You look like hell," he said, walking toward her, barely giving her time to recover or react in any way.

She tucked a strand of her hair behind her ear, fervently wishing she'd washed it and worn something other than faded sweatpants and the thick, chunky sweater made out of Italian wool—the one thing she had stolen from him. But she'd been acting on instinct, urged on by a reckless kind of desperation. She'd needed to see him.

The closer he came, though, the less panicky and anxious she felt. Almost as if she couldn't be anything less near this man than her whole self, this man who had taught her that she deserved everything she ever wanted in life—including his love. Straightening her shoulders, she lifted her chin. "I haven't been doing well." When he scowled, she sighed and added, "Emotionally, I mean."

"But you're well enough to come into my home and rifle through my things? What were you planning to steal?"

"I'm not stealing anything. There are a couple of things I left and they're mine," she bluffed.

"Like what?"

"Like the necklace you picked for me."

"Why do you want it when you didn't want me?"

Outrage erupted from her mouth like an indignant squeak. "I never said I didn't want you. I never even said I was ending it. You did. I just wanted some space. I needed to know that what I felt for you was different from what I felt for Francesco. For that I needed to grow up, understand my own needs and wants first. In the end, it turned out to be right."

He was closer now and she could smell that delicious scent of his and feel that warmth of his body, and her knees nearly buckled.

"What turned out to be right, *bella*?" he said with an infinite tenderness, and this close, Monica could see that he had not fared any better than her at all. There was a gaunt, downright pinched, look to his features as if something dark had etched itself permanently onto them. Her loss, she wanted to think, though it didn't really give her solace. He looked ravaged, reduced, less of that vibrant, energetic man she knew and adored. "What did your little experiment prove, except that it made us both miserable?"

She swallowed at the rough rasp of his voice as he asked that, as if he, too, was making an effort to speak past the pain. And this new, brave, not-delusional version of her knew, in her gut, that he *was* in pain. That he had missed her as much as she'd missed him or even more. Because when Andrea Valentini gave something, he gave it with his whole heart. And that gave her the courage to say all that was in her own. "It proved that I am in love with you, that these feelings I have for you—" she rubbed at her chest, feeling actual pain there "—are so real that you're all I think of and see and feel even when I'm not near you. It proved that what I thought I felt for Francesco was nothing more than a cheap imitation of the real thing. What I feel for you, Andrea, it makes me braver, stronger, makes me know myself like I never did before. It makes me want the best for myself. So it also proved that I'd have been miserable to marry you without having your love."

"If I talk about my grief about Papa, if I tell you of myself at my worst moment, then, *bella*?"

"I already know you blame yourself for that accident. That for months after, you wouldn't look at Flora. That you and Romeo nearly lost each other all over again. I know that it has only driven you to be a better man, a man your father would have been proud of. Whatever you think is your worst, Andrea, I only love even more."

"And yet instead of facing me, you return to Italy, work for my brother right under my nose? What is that, *bella*?"

It took her a moment, looking around the shifting light in the room—suddenly they were cocooned in a thick darkness—to realize he had gotten even closer. With his arm on the wall behind her head, he had caged her in, and yet it felt so natural that if they were in a room together, any room, it was impossible that they would stay apart. Something about his tone made her tilt her chin up and look into his eyes. He had known she was back, that she was working for Romeo. The little flicker of hope in her heart turned into a bright, glowing flame. "It was *your* idea that I work for Romeo. Your idea that I stay with his girlfriend. Even my return ticket, you arranged it through him."

"*Si.*"

"Why? So that I can feel even more indebted to you? So that you can flex your power over me?"

"Is that what you truly think, Monica?" he said, his breath warm on her cheek.

She turned and their mouths were so close that she could feel the weight and depth of his lips crashing over hers. She wanted to touch him and kiss him so badly that she was trembling with the need. And the truth was plainly written in his gaze if only she was brave enough to see it. "You… You wanted me to have that safe space. You wanted me to prove to myself that I'm strong enough to come back and face you. You wanted me to have the security of knowing that Romeo and Flora are not lost to me. That you're not lost to me, even outside of our relationship."

"*Si.*"

A sob threatened to burst through her chest. Monica bunched her fists against his chest, the sensation of his skin against her fingers nearly burning her. "Why? Why do all that for me? Why?"

"You have a pretty logical brain, *bella*. Why don't you follow through?"

"I can follow the logic, yes," she said, smiling through her tears. "But I need to hear you say it, Andrea. All my life, I was desperate to belong somewhere, to be wanted. So desperate that somewhere came to mean anywhere. But not anymore. With you, I need so much more. With you, I want the entire world. I want…" She pressed her hand to his chest and felt the thundering beat of his heart. "I want…your words, because I know you don't give them lightly."

He smiled then and she could see his heart in it. "Flexing your claws again?"

"With you, yes. Since I know you love them," she said, gaining back some of her own spirit.

His gray gaze held hers then, his hands taking hers. He opened his mouth and closed it a couple of times, as if words couldn't encompass what he felt. God, she had always understood him best, better than anyone.

Finally, when he spoke, his words were low and soft and full of his love. "My heart, my body, my everything, is yours, Monica. I'm so sorry it took me so long to see what I have in you, to realize how much I already needed you. You didn't just change me, *bella*, you brought me back to life. You completed me even before I knew what that meant."

When Monica had imagined this moment, and she had over the past few weeks with a feverish, desperate urgency, she was laughing and screaming with joy. But reality was different. Even hearing those words from him only brought into keener contrast all the doubts and ache she'd suffered, all the anguish of wondering if he'd ever choose this between them, if he'd ever choose *her*.

"To wait for you to come to me, to hope that you would see you belong with me and I with you…has been the hardest thing I've ever done in life. I will give you words and actions and promises and presents, if only you give me one chance, *bella*. I will give you all of myself."

And then she could hold off no longer. She pressed her mouth to his, half sobbing, half yelling and the shape and taste of him started a riot in her body. He clamped her hard to him, his fingers digging almost painfully into her hips as he devoured her mouth. It was a hard, rough, possessive kind of kiss and it was exactly what she needed.

He bit her lower lip, licked the hurt and repeated the rough caresses over and over again. Shaking and gasping, Monica clung to him, rubbing herself against his body. "I need to be inside you, *bella*," he whispered, his words taking on a guttural slant, his urgency in every touch.

"Yes, now, please," she said.

He pushed her sweatpants down roughly and she

kicked them off, and when he lifted her, she wrapped her legs around his waist. Pressing her back against the wall, he thrust inside her and Monica banged her head into the wall and he cursed and cradled her head, but the jarring pain of it only made the pleasure in her lower belly even more white-hot.

But she didn't want to miss an inch of this, so she clasped his cheek and looked at him and when he said, "Say it again," she shouted the words instead.

"I love you, Andrea!" She repeated his name again and again, on each silken thrust, and soon, she burst like a star in the sky and he was following her.

And even though she'd come to accept that the future was uncertain, Monica knew she'd never regret a moment spent with him. Not when it was true that he loved her, too.

It felt like hours but it was only minutes later, after they had both washed up and she was in his lap in his armchair, that Andrea was able to hear his heart's muted whispers again.

It was only now, when he could physically touch her and feel her weight in his arms, that he felt like his world was all right again. Her cheek pressed to his heart, Monica burrowed into him as if she never wanted to leave again.

"Tell me, Andrea. I know your heart but still, I want to hear it. Please."

He tilted her chin up and looking into those beautiful yellow eyes, Andrea saw his future. "I'm in love with you, *bella*. I knew it even as you shouted it at me. I knew as I walked away from you. But I couldn't face it. All I could see was pain and loss ahead, even as I was already losing you. So young as you are, what you did was right for both of us. It was only after losing you that I could see why it was so easy for me to jump into a compromise of a marriage. You were right. I was cheating you. And I was cheating myself."

"You still want to marry me, then?" she asked, her voice small and fragile, and he felt as if she could turn him inside out.

"*Si*. More than anything in the world. I want to have you all to myself first. Then I want to have a family with you, if that's what you want. And I want to love you every day for the rest of our lives. You changed me even before you were my fake fiancée, *bella*. And I can't wait to see what else life holds for us."

Then she was crying and whispering, "Yes, I'll marry you," and Andrea kissed her and tasted her tears and her pain and her love and vowed to himself that she'd never doubt herself or his love ever again.

* * * * *

   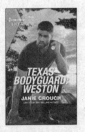